M000308190

A RedSage Publishing Publication

Information:
Red Sage Publishing, Inc. P.O. Box 4844 Seminole, FL 33775
727-391-3847 eRedSage.com

Forbidden Fruit & Reckless Exposure

An eRedSage Publication All Rights Reserved Copyright © 2010

eRedSage is a registered trademark of Red Sage Publishing, Inc.
Visit us on the World Wide Web: http://www.eRedSage.com

ISBN: 978-1-60310-583-5; 1-60310-583-2
Forbidden Fruit & Reckless Exposure, print version

Book layout and typesetting by jimandzetta.com
Cover © 2010 by Rae Monet, Inc.

Printed in the U.S.A.

Forbidden

Fruit

To My Reader:

It's a pleasure for me to create less than perfect heroines that are easy to relate to and I especially had fun with Ava Sweet. She's one tough lady, but with a soft center. She deserved a hunky bad boy to show her just how beautiful she is. I dearly hope you enjoy Ava's transformation from shy tomboy to sexy siren!

-Anne Rainey

Forbidden Fruit: Chapter 1

"Oh god, what am I even doing here? I don't belong here!"

Jen took Ava by the shoulders and gave her a shake. "Remember Monday? Standing on Luke's front porch and hearing every awful word that fell out of his big dumb mouth?"

Ava remembered. It hurt, but she remembered.

She'd gone to Luke's on Monday because he'd found a cat on his front porch and hadn't a clue as to what to do with it. Inches from the screen door, she stopped dead at the words that drifted out to her.

***

"Since when do you have the hots for my sister's friend?"

"I wouldn't say I have the hots for her, but there's no denying that she's one sexy piece of ass, Luke."

"Dr. Doolittle? Sexy?"

He sounded so incredulous and Ava felt her heart sink.

"Hell, yes, sexy!" At that moment, she could have planted one on Pete's lips for that manly comment. "I'd give my left nut to see that curvy ass of hers in the buff.

It's all heart-shaped and... just so damned squeezable."

Luke, the idiot, dug himself in deeper. "Are we talking about the same woman here?"

Pete just plowed on, oblivious that Luke wasn't buying a word he was saying. "And those magnificent tits. Just right, ya know? All soft and bouncy and round. I swear to Christ I don't think she owns a single bra."

"How can you tell what her ass or her tits look like when every piece of clothing she owns is big and baggy and ugly as sin?"

Her shoulders slumped. That confirmed her worst fears. Luke would never see her as a woman. Only ever as the plain tomboy, animal lover friend of his sister, Jen.

Great.

"You don't need to have x-ray vision, Luke. Ava Sweet isn't all fluff and makeup, true, but, she's real and everything a man could want in a woman. She has natural beauty. The kind most women envy. And I'd bet money that beneath those baggy clothes is one helluva woman just waiting for a man to sink his teeth in."

"But, again, I ask you, how the hell can you even tell? She's all bulky cotton material! And that hair. I don't think I've ever seen it out of that nasty ass ponytail she wears day in and day out."

Can you blame her?"

"What do mean?"

"She probably dresses like that to deter her boss and every other man she comes across."

"What does her boss have to do with it?"

Yeah, that's what she'd like to know.

"I've been to the clinic where she works and I've seen the good doc giving her the once over. If she came to work looking all... girly, he'd be on her quicker than a cat to cream."

"You've been to her clinic?"

"Yep."

"What the hell for? You don't even own a pet."

"Jesus, Luke, for such a ladies man you can be real dense sometimes."

Enough was enough, Ava decided. Time to retrieve the cat and give Luke a piece of her mind in the process.

Without waiting to hear anymore of Luke's cutting remarks, Ava swung the screen wide and strode right in. Both men turned to her with twin-horrified expressions on their handsome faces. Ava didn't waver. She asked where the cat was and Luke showed her to the backyard. The poor cat was on the brink of starvation. Judging by the bowl of food on the porch, Luke had apparently been trying to fatten the poor thing up. But one look and Ava knew the neglected animal would need to be looked over by her boss, Dr. Ryan.

She moved slowly towards the scared orange tabby

and picked her up, nearly crying when she felt the animal's ribs. She made soft, reassuring sounds to her and went back into the house. But she didn't head for the front door. Instead, she sat the cat gently on the floor, walked right up to Pete, and kissed him.

On the mouth.

Tongue and all.

Pete reached out and placed his palms on her head, holding her still while he plunged and ate at her mouth. She pulled back finally, breathless and shocked that she'd done something so brazen. Shocked that Pete had let her.

"Friday night, seven o'clock. You and me." Ava demanded, not bothering to play the shy schoolgirl. She just wasn't cut out for it.

For a minute, Pete just stared at her, as if trying to figure her angle and then he whispered, "Anything you want, darlin'."

She nodded briskly and then went to Luke. His gaze was a mixture of anger and surprise. Ava was pleased. She smiled at him and his eyes narrowed. Then she brought her knee to his groin. Hard. Luke's smile disappeared as he fell to the floor, cursing.

"Pete's right, you can be real dense sometimes, Luke McGiffin."

Then she'd picked the cat back up and left. Her body vibrating with rage and hurt and even fear. Fear that she'd never be able to get over her infatuation for a man that viewed her as nothing more than an oddity.

***

It was now Thursday and they had a full day ahead of them. She nodded to her friend, grabbed the few articles of clothing Jen had picked out for her, and groused, "Fine then, let's do this thing."

A few minutes later, Ava was looking in the mirror of the tiny dressing room. The woman staring back at her was a stranger. She didn't even recognize herself. Amazing the difference a few scraps of material could make. And that's all they were too, a few very small scraps of material.

She shored up her nerve and swung open the curtain. "Well, what do you think?"

Jen stared, her jaw dropping, eyes bugging out. She stared for so long it made Ava snap out, "If you can't even form a coherent sentence then it must be even more horrid than I thought!" She threw her hands up and started back into the dressing room.

Finally, Jen found her voice.

"My lord in heaven, Ava. You look absolutely gorgeous. I really had no idea."

That had her stopping and turning. "Gee, thanks, Jen," Ava said ruefully and planted her hands on her hips.

Jen shook her head and beamed a smile at her. "No, what I mean is, I knew you had a body under all that material, but lordy that skirt looks fabulous on you.

Luke is going to swallow his tongue when he sees you, I can promise you that. I know my brother, Ava. He'll stop, he'll stare, and then he'll pounce." Then Jen's brows drew together in concern. "As a matter of fact. Pete may just do the same thing."

Ava shook her head in denial of that statement, before looking down at the white skirt. She tugged at the hem, willing it to grow another inch. She'd never felt comfortable with her thighs showing. Not even in the dead of summer. It made her feel vulnerable and gangly. Somehow, it just seemed too intimate to have that much flesh on display. She was a throwback to the old spinster days, that's what she was. And she'd never get Luke's attention if she continued acting the maiden.

"We made a deal, Jen," Ava reminded her best bud. "I'm going to get Pete to the nightclub, but you are going to be the one to knock his socks off."

Ava knew that Jen had been enthralled by Pete for a long time. Maybe not as long as she'd been taken with Luke, but long enough. Jen was just too shy to make the first move. Apparently, Pete was too. Ava didn't tell Jen that Pete had a thing for her. She, however, had seen the signs. Anytime Jen and Pete were in the same room together, Pete watched her. Stalked her with his eyes. Jen couldn't stub a toe without Pete taking notice. But she knew Jen too well. If she had any inkling Pete wanted her she would back out. No, Friday night, Ava would get the pair in the same room together and let instincts and pheromones take it from there.

"Well, I know for sure my brother is going to be begging your forgiveness the instant he sets his sights on you in that outfit, Ava."

She turned again and looked into the three-way mirror, seeing her reflection from every possible angle. The white skirt was clingy and short and undoubtedly sexy. Good thing she was in decent shape. All the time she spent going up to the high school, jogging the track before heading to work was now paying off.

The pale pink silk blouse with its scooped neckline and billowy sleeves was just enough enhancement too. Not overblown, but quiet and delicate and feminine. And that was the plan, wasn't it? To look, girly? She'd never attempted that sort of thing. From the time she was big enough to walk, she'd been a tomboy. She had played sports in school, had hung with the guys, and was more comfortable changing her own oil as opposed to watching demurely from the sidelines as some macho mechanic did it for her. And yet, she'd somehow made fast friends with the head of the cheerleading squad, Jen McGiffin.

Ava was a senior in high school when the McGiffin's had moved to town. Jen with her sweet smile and pretty, blond hair had nothing in common with her brother. Where Jen was the good girl who'd gotten straight A's, Luke was the bad boy who'd been held back a grade, putting him in the same classes as his sister, ten months his junior.

The rebel with the dark hair and leather jacket and fast car. She'd melted the first time she'd seen him. Luke had walked into their school, strode straight up to the most popular girl at Green Valley High, and kissed her. Then he'd asked her out. The popular, Heather, along with every other girl in school, had panted after him like little lost puppies. Ava had stomped off, making fun of the simpering little fools. But deep down, in the most secret part of her soul, she'd been the same as those girls. She'd just been too afraid to admit it. And where had that gotten her? At a fancy boutique, trying on outfit after outfit in the hopes of gaining the attention of the biggest playboy and rebel that Green Valley, Ohio had ever seen.

Whom was she kidding?

Once again, she covered her face and moaned like a wimp. "I cannot believe I'm doing this, Jen!" she felt Jen's comforting hand on her back, patting and soothing. "I'm not cut out to be a vixen!"

Jen laughed. "Of course you are, hon. Every woman on the face of the earth was born with an inner vixen. She just needs to tap into her. Which is why we're here. It's also why you're going to go get your hair done, a facial, manicure, and pedicure."

When she put it that way, she almost wanted to hide under a rock. Ava had never painted her fingernails. And she'd certainly never had someone kneeling at her feet to apply color to her toes. It would probably tickle. She sighed and knew a new determination she'd never felt before. Tickling or not, she'd get her stupid hair done, her nails would have color and she'd walk into that nightclub ready for battle, armor and all!

"You know what, Jen? You're right. Let's get this over with so I can give Luke a taste of what he's been missing all these damn years."

"Now that's the spirit!" Jen shouted, getting all giddy and excited, as only a former cheerleader could.

And so the day went. First the clothes. Then the hair. Last came the tickling pedi and mani. Ava had been surprised to find out that she'd actually enjoyed herself. At the hair salon, the stylist had suggested they put in a few subtle highlights and trim the split-ends. Ava's hair was healthy and full, but it needed a bit of this and that, Rhonda had explained. By the time, the bouncy woman was done Ava was beyond nervous. But when she saw the finished product, she'd been shocked. Mostly because she wasn't much different. Just... better somehow. Rhonda had uncovered something that Ava had never known was even there. Her hair fairly shone. The cut was perfect with long layers all around her face. No curling needed, Rhonda had instructed. Just a hair dryer and a round brush, which Ava had purchased at the salon. Jen had been thrilled with the look. A good sign, since Jen was a pro when it came to fashion.

Next came the nails. Jen had politely explained that

Ava had never colored her nails and to do so now, might be too much. Instead, the nail tech had gone for a French manicure. It seemed to make her hands look softer, more fragile. Ava had never in her life felt soft or fragile. It was a new, and somewhat uncomfortable, feeling. Still, she liked that her nails weren't shouting, "Hey, look at me!" Instead they seemed to quietly whisper, "don't I look pretty?"

Now, Ava was home and resting her feet. She hadn't known beauty could be so damned exhausting. She took a sip from her white wine and stared at all her new clothes. "I cannot believe I actually did it." What was she supposed to do with it all? She'd spent more money than she'd ever spent on any single car part or workout gear. And for what? For Luke McGiffin. If the man didn't sit up and take notice now, he never would.

"He damn well better be worth the trouble," she muttered.

Tomorrow was Friday. Her big début, as it were. She took another sip of her wine and looked again at the white skirt and pink top. She let out a sigh, laid her head back against the soft brown leather of the chair and let her mind drift. She imagined Luke striding up to her on the dance floor. Grabbing her by the shoulders and kissing her. Rough and demanding. Kissing the way a man kissed a woman that he ached for. That he wanted to claim and conquer. And wasn't that a hoot! Ava Sweet, track star, basketball MVP of

Green Valley High, wanting to be conquered.

The phone rang, startling her out of her wild and impossible dreams.

She reached over and picked up her black cordless. "Hello?"

"Hey."

Ava nearly choked on her wine. "Luke?"

Silence and then, "Yeah, it's me."

His deep, husky drawl nearly did her in. She could always feel that dark timbre clear to her toes, as well as all the places in between. "Uh, hi."

"Hi, Ava."

Ava? What was that about? "What, no Dr. Doolittle this time, Luke?"

"Tomorrow's your night with Pete."

Her heart did a little flip at the way he said Pete's name—as if it left a funny taste in his mouth. Jealousy?

"Yea, tomorrow's our date. Jen took me shopping today for it."

She thought she heard him emit a low growl, just before saying, "Yeah, she told me all about your fun day together." He paused and added, "She mentioned that you bought a few new things."

How much did Jen say? She wasn't supposed to tell him anything, darn it! She should have known. After all, they were brother and sister. And they were as close as twins.

"Actually, yeah, I did buy a few new things," she

confirmed, then she teased a little more by adding, "I think Pete is going to really enjoy my outfit tomorrow night."

"Pete seems to like you no matter what you're wearing," Luke grumbled. "So, what did you buy for good ol' Pete?"

Darn, if he didn't sound jealous! Could it be possible? It'd mean she meant something to him. Something more than Dr. Doolittle anyway. "I bought a mini skirt." She wouldn't tell him about the hair and the shoes. Or what she bought to wear under the skirt.

She heard him cough. Hard. As if having a spasm. "Luke? Are you okay?"

A couple more very tense seconds of coughs, and then, "Did you say a skirt?"

She wanted to smack him. "Yes, Luke. It's this tiny, stretchy thing with a zipper on the side that women wear when they want to look sexy. You may have seen one or two."

"I know what a skirt is. Quit being so damned sarcastic, damn it. What I'm trying to figure out is why the hell you have one?"

Now that rankled. "You know, it occurs to me that just because you see me as this ugly, sexless, animal-lover type doesn't mean that every man sees me in the same light. Some men find me attractive. Go figure!"

She wanted to slam the phone down, but then she heard him say, "I never said you were ugly and sexless,

Ava."

"No, you just said that I'm all bulky cotton and have an ugly-ass ponytail."

Silence.

"Luke?"

"I'm sorry," Luke muttered. "I shouldn't have said that, but it took me by surprise to have Pete seeing you that way."

"What way?"

"He noticed you. Your body, your softness. I thought I'd been the only guy to see that. To see past the clothes and to the woman beneath."

Oh God, she'd never survive if he kept saying such things. She'd waited years to hear sweet words like that from Luke. "To be honest, it felt good to have Pete see me as soft and sweet and sexy. Not like an oddity."

"You were always so standoffish, Ava." Luke explained, once again in defensive mode. "You acted like you hated being around me. I thought..."

His words trailed off and suddenly Ava was riveted. She wanted to hear the rest of this Thursday night confession. "You thought what? That I wasn't a woman with a woman's needs?"

"No. I thought you saw me as some macho badass rebel and I didn't want you to see me that way. I wanted you to see me. The *real* me."

She sighed, wondering if they would ever get past the misconceptions they had of each other. "That makes two of us, Luke."

"There are two things I want you to know before you go out on your date with Pete tomorrow night."

"And what might they be?"

"I never meant the Dr. Doolittle comment to be insulting. I love that you care for animals, Ava. It screams sensitivity. You're a nurturer and that's something I've always admired in you. I don't think you're odd either. I think you're lovable as hell. And I'm damned glad no one else calls you Dr. Doolittle. That's for me and me alone." Luke paused and in a much colder tone he added, "If Pete touches you, kisses you, dances too fucking close to you, I'll beat the shit out of him, Ava. I swear it. He's my best friend in the world, but I will not be happy if he touches you. Think about that when you're out on your date with him, baby. Think long and hard. You know me. I don't issue silly threats. Only promises that I mean to keep."

Then the line went dead and Ava was left holding a cold piece of plastic, her mouth gaping wide. Had he really just threatened bodily harm to his best friend? And all because of her? What on earth did that mean?

Ava trembled.

She took a long gulp of her wine, draining the glass. She wasn't cut out for a man like Luke. What had she done?

Oh God, what on earth had she done?

Forbidden Fruit: Chapter 2

Luke hung up the phone and ran a hand through his hair. He was on the very edge of going to Ava's house and fucking her brains out.

"Shit!"

He shot out of his chair and paced the room. He'd always had a hard time keeping his relationship with Ava platonic. He'd taken one look at her back in high school and knew she was too wild to ever be tamed. Too independent and headstrong. So, he'd done the right thing. He'd backed off and let her have free rein.

Now, ten years later, at twenty-seven years old, she was spitting mad and ready to prove her womanhood— or whatever the hell it was women did when they felt their femininity threatened. There was no telling what she'd end up doing with Pete. Something she'd regret later, no doubt. If she touched him, took him home and stripped out of those damned awful clothes she insisted on wearing, Luke would make Pete regret ever having been born.

She'd been a fascination to him for far too long. He'd tried to see her as just a friend of his sister. An odd little creature who loved animals. Giving her the Dr. Doolittle title had been a way for him to create distance between them. But nothing had worked. She'd still managed to slip inside his dreams. Inside his fantasies. He'd had his fair share of hot and sweaty nights. More than once he'd taken his cock in his hand and pumped himself to completion as he thought of what he wanted to do to her. In the dark privacy, where no one could see or know what he was thinking, it'd been Ava's face he'd imagined kissing. Her mouth he pictured sucking him.

What would her body look like? How perky and fresh would her tits be? The color of her nipples. The taste and feel of her pussy against his hungry mouth. How sweet she'd be when he swallowed her honey. He knew it in his bones. She'd be a tight fist around his dick when he entered her the first time. Her body would accept his cock, because she was made for him and no other man. Certainly not Pete.

As he went to the refrigerator and grabbed a cold bottle of beer, Luke smiled. Little Ava was wrong on all counts. She'd never had the slightest inkling that he'd ejaculated into the shower drain a hundred times, as he thought of fucking her in every position imaginable. Wishing it were her tight cunt instead of his hand.

Luke placed his beer on the kitchen table, then picked up the phone and dialed another number. When he heard the deep voice of his best friend, Luke said the first thing that came to mind.

"What the hell do you think you're doing, Pete?"

Pete was silent, probably wondering if he'd gone nuts. Hell, maybe he had. "Huh?"

"She's not some little twit you can manipulate and toy with. She's a nice girl. You never go out with nice girls. So, I'll ask again. What the fuck do you think you're doing?"

"Maybe I've changed my mind," Pete taunted. "I told you I always suspected that Ava would be a sweet piece of ass underneath it all."

Luke had heard enough of what Pete thought of Ava's body. So there was no misunderstandings, Luke explained in very clear terms what he *wouldn't* be doing come Friday night.

"You touch her and our friendship is over. Ava is off limits."

Pete laughed, as if he hadn't a care in the world. "What's it to you? She's only your sister's friend. Right?"

And there it was. Pete had him by the short hairs and they both knew it. Luke shook off the unsettling notion that Ava was becoming way more than just a fascination to him.

"Just know that I'm not screwing around here. Keep your hands to yourself." With that threat hanging between them, Luke hung up the phone and began mentally rearranging his Friday night schedule. No matter where Pete took Ava, Luke was going to be there, watching every move they made. Ava had run wild long enough. It was time to tug on the reins.

***

Once more, tomboy Ava was standing in front of a mirror inspecting herself. Or *dissecting* herself. Yeah, that was closer to the truth. Even though she was going out with Pete, a friend she had no romantic feelings for whatsoever, it still felt real. He was a dear man. Hard working. Gorgeous. And he'd be seeing her for the first time in the soft, feminine clothes. Legs, heels, minuscule skirt and all. He'd be the very first man to ever see Ava Sweet as a woman. A curvy and hopefully sensual woman. Somehow, it made her sad. She wanted Luke to be the one at her door. She wanted Luke to see her wearing her very first skirt ever.

But, it wasn't to be that way. And Ava didn't spend time on what should be. She made her own way and dealt with what she had at her disposal. And tonight, she'd be greeting Pete Redding. He'd take her arm and gentlemanly escort her to the, Shake A Leg, Luke's favorite hangout. Jen swore he'd be there with his buddies, drinking and laughing. Hopefully Ava would be able to walk straight and tall and not trip and fall like some ninny. Ava looked down at her shoes and wondered if she should change them. They were white strappy sandals. The straps laced up her ankle and Jen had sworn to her that it was a very sensual style. That it made her look alluring.

Ava hoped to God she didn't fall flat on her ass.

"That would certainly ruin the whole alluring part."
Then she heard her doorbell chime.

"Crap!" this was really happening. Her date was here
and she was going to see Luke. In a skirt!
"Ohgodohgodohgod!" She smacked her cheeks once,
twice, and then stated, "This is no different than the
State Finals in track. I won that and I'll damn well win
this too."

The doorbell chimed again and she left the
bathroom behind and opened her front door. "Hi!" she
said a bit too cheerfully. Pete, on the other hand, didn't
say a darn thing. He just stood there. Staring. He had
that same shell-shocked look that Jen had gotten at the
boutique. It made her grit her teeth.

"I swear, if one more person gives me that, 'oh wow,
you really are a chick!' look I'll punch them square in
the eye."

"Uh, right. I, well, that is... fuck," Pete muttered, as
he scrubbed a hand over his face.

Oh, well, that was a bit different from what Jen had
said. She struck what she thought looked like a
provocative pose and teased, "You think I look okay?"

Pete snorted. "I think you look hot. Really hot."

She didn't want Pete having any illusions about
tonight. Time to explain the real reason behind the
date. "Pete, I sort of... know how you feel about Jen."

Pete turned red. "I'm that obvious?"

Ava shook her head. "Not at all. In fact, Jen has no

clue."

"Good, let's keep it that way."

"The thing is, she's going to be at the Shake A Leg tonight. I thought maybe..."

"You thought maybe we could each finally get what we want." An ornery smile played at the corners of his mouth.

"Something like that."

He looked her over again and whistled. "Luke is going to be equal parts pissed off and turned-on when he sees you in that getup, darlin'."

"Pissed?"

"He's really not going to like knowing that you're on my arm this evening." Pete had a wicked gleam in his eye. He was clearly looking forward to making Luke jealous. But Ava remembered Luke's warning and it made her just a touch nervous to think what Luke might do if Pete pushed too hard.

Should she warn Pete? Nah—she wouldn't let it worry her.

Time to have some fun. She had a plan and she intended to make it work. Knowing that Jen was waiting and hoping to see Pete helped calm her jumpy nerves. Ava wasn't the only one putting her heart on the line. The thought made her feel immensely better.

Luke would see her as a sensual, passionate woman if it killed her. Thinking of only that, she announced, "I believe it's time to make the McGiffins squirm." She held out her arm. "Shall we?"

Pete winked and twined her arm through his. "Hell of an idea, Ava. Hell of an idea."

***

Ava walked into Shake A Leg on the arm of her handsome blonde escort, stomach clenching in her anxiety. Her face heated at the interested glances that swung her way from some of the men in the darkly lit room. The D.J. was pounding to the rhythm of, Sweet Cherry Pie, by Warrant. There was something about the erotic tune that made her confidence level rise a notch. Ava stood a little straighter as she scanned the crowded room, looking every which way for Jen, while at the same time searching for Luke.

"Luke is here tonight, right?"

"Yep. Griff called to tell me they were coming and asked if I wanted to join them."

Ava cringed. Griff was the biggest playboy and womanizer of the bunch. He'd take one look at her and think he could score. If she escaped this night without having to land a punch to the gut or a knee to the groin it'd be a miracle.

Then she saw Luke and she knew he saw her, too, because he'd stopped listening to Griff. His eyes were now pinning her in place. She felt the full blast of his attention and all that masculine focus on her for the first time ever. Ava swayed on her feet a bit under his intense male perusal, her body going liquid as his eyes roamed from head to toe and then back again. Thankfully, Pete was there to grab her, otherwise she would have landed on her butt, exactly as she'd envisioned.

He looked so good. So ruggedly masculine in a pair of old, worn jeans, clean black work boots, and a black t-shirt that had something printed in big white letters across the front. He'd even attempted to tame the wild mane of his dark hair, not that it did much good, as it was every bit as ruffled as ever. Still, his jeans held all her attention. They cupped the heavy weight of his sex in the most delicious way. She could easily imagine herself on her knees in front of him, unzipping his fly and watching in fascination as his cock sprang free of the tight confines.

Luke moved then, startling her out of her fantasy, his hungry eyes all over her at once. Pete immediately stepped away from her. It was a subtle few inches and if she hadn't been so aware, she would have missed it. With a smile and a wink, Pete was letting her know that it was okay, that she could do this. Unfortunately, he had more confidence in her than she did. Good lord, even from a distance, the pounding music, the crushing bodies she could still see Luke's intent.

He wanted her.

Nothing and no one would stop him from getting to her either.

Ava wavered. She wasn't girly enough to handle a

man like Luke McGiffin. He was all predatory male and she was, Ava—animal lover.

"I have to go to the little girl's room, Pete."

Pete stared down at her and gave her a knowing smile, then leaned towards her so he could be heard over the music. "You're nervous. Its okay, Ava. It's natural to be anxious after such a dramatic change." She started to protest, not willing to own up to anything so weak, but then he was plowing right over her. "I'm nervous too. And you can bet that Luke is nervous as hell right now."

Ava looked over at Luke, he was still heading towards her, but women kept stopping him. One woman even went so far as to step directly into his path.

Damn hussy.

Ava flung her hair back and muttered, "Funny, he certainly doesn't look nervous to me."

Pete saw the woman standing in Luke's path and his friend's attempt to wave her away. "Aw, that ain't nothing. Luke gets that sort of thing all the time."

She looked up at Pete with murder in her eyes. "And that's supposed to make me feel all warm and cozy inside?"

Pete had the good grace to flush.

"It doesn't matter anyway. I don't care one way or the other. Luke can have the silly little piece of fluff for all I care. I'm here to have a good time." She held out her hand and demanded, "Take me out to the dance floor."

Pete looked at Luke, then back at her, and then proceeded to rub the back of his neck. "Uh, I'm not sure that's a good idea, Ava."

Ava planted her hands on her hips and all but shouted. "Why not? I'm not going to let these clothes go to waste. I spent good, hard-earned money to look nice for tonight. Now you can either dance with me or I'll find someone else more willing."

"Alright! Don't go getting all feral on me." Then he grabbed her hand and tugged her onto the dance floor. The fast beat had changed to a softer, slower tune. Pete took her in his arms, then leaned in to whisper, "Just so you know though, Luke's going to pound me a good one. If I look all gross and bloody Jen's never going to want to go out with me. It'll be all your fault too."

If Ava weren't so mad at Luke, she would have smiled at that statement. Going up on her tiptoes, she whispered right back, "Don't you know that women love to pamper an injured man, Pete? The blood will only have Jen running to your rescue." She could practically feel Pete's excitement at that prospect. But before he could say anything more, a tap on Pete's shoulder interrupted them. Pete turned around and that's when Ava was able to see Griff behind him. She wanted to groan. As she scanned the crowd and saw Luke with the hussy still, her heart squeezed tight. She hated to see him with other women. It nearly killed her every awful time.

"May I have this dance?"

Pete looked at Ava for his cue. She shrugged. "Why not? I'm at a hot and trendy nightclub and I even wore a skirt and heels. I'm not going to let it go to waste."

Pete frowned, his lips thinning angrily. Reluctantly, he stepped aside, giving Griff enough room to step up and take her in his arms. Which he did. Unfortunately, he wasn't content to leave a little space, as Pete had done. Griff pulled her in tight. Too tight.

Griff wasn't a bad looking man; he was just too much of a chauvinistic ass for her to want anything to do with him. She never did understand his association with Luke. They seemed like opposites to her. Oh sure, they both loved to play the field, but that was where the similarities ended in her way of thinking. Then she felt Griff slide his hand down her back to her waistline, and then below. He leaned down and she could smell the alcohol on his breath when he said, "You look good enough to eat, Ava."

She shuddered. She reached around the back of her and placed her hand over his. "Don't let the skirt fool you, Griff. I will make you sing like a little choir girl if you don't lift your hand right now."

"I can vouch for that," came a deadly sounding voice from behind her. She turned slowly, knowing who that voice belonged to and not in too big a hurry to see the owner after what she'd done on Monday. Just as she suspected, he was good and pissed. His fists were clenched at his side, nostrils flaring; Luke looked like an angry bull ready to charge.

"I'm cutting in," Luke stated in a voice as hard as granite. Griff, the drunken idiot, merely grinned and stepped out of the way.

Ava crossed her arms over her chest. She was still fuming over all the women she'd had to witness coming on to Luke. "What if I don't want to dance with you?"

Luke stepped forward, crowding her, making her feel tiny in comparison to his much larger frame. "Too damn bad, because you aren't dancing with any other guy tonight. I can promise you that, Ava. It's me or no one."

Ava wanted to protest. To toss out a few sarcastic comments, and then stomp off. But, her eyes went to his shirt and she read the white lettering across the front.

"Get Nailed, Lay a Roof-er?" she read aloud, her voice sounding prudish and shrill.

He did that grin and wink thing that always had her going mute, and then Luke's arm came around her waist. He pulled her tight against him and suddenly Ava couldn't think of a single snide thing to say.

God, she'd imagined this whole scenario. Wanted so badly to be in his arms. To feel all that hard, ruthless strength against her flesh for so many lonely years. It

31

was like coming home. Her body began to sway to the beat, moving in harmony with his, as if made for each other. When she felt his breath against her cheek, lips just barely grazing over her skin, Ava quivered. Heat pooled low in her belly. She'd never felt a reaction so swift and all consuming. Only with Luke. He was the only man to make her ache this way. The only man to make her want to hand over all control.

It was a scary feeling.

Forbidden Fruit: Chapter 3

"You look incredible, Ava. Every man in this room wanted you the instant you walked through those doors. Including me, baby."

Ava forced herself not to react to the heat and promise in his words. She had a few questions for him before things went too far.

Pushing back enough so she could look into his eyes, Ava nearly swallowed her tongue. He was so tall and she was all of five foot four. He made her feel more feminine than any skirt ever could. She pulled herself out of her wayward thoughts and asked, "What about the woman I saw you with a few minutes ago? Do you want her too?"

He frowned down at her, as if he had no idea who she was talking about. "Huh?"

Ava rolled her eyes. "Don't tell me you don't know! She practically flung herself at you." He still looked bewildered, so she added, "Blonde. Tall. A chest that looks like maybe it's been under a knife."

Ah, there it was. Recognition at last. Mention boobs and a man's memory suddenly became crystal clear. She wanted to smack him. She wanted to kiss him. Maybe she'd do both before the night was through.

"First off, I wasn't *with* her. She came onto me. I turned her down. She's not the woman that has my dick as hard as a damned tire iron right now, Ava; that would be you."

She stubbornly ignored the erection pressing against her belly—or tried to anyway—and narrowed her eyes on him. Luke wasn't a one-woman man. He liked variety. A fact that had left her feeling raw on more than one occasion.

"Maybe she's not the one you want right now, but I'm betting you jotted down her phone number." She needed to know. At the very least, Ava needed to know that she was going to have his full attention tonight. If only for one night. Ava badly wanted to experience the whole of Luke McGiffin. Preferably before reality came crashing back in on her with all its merciless force.

"I told her I wasn't interested. She wrote her number on my hand by her own volition, but I went to the bathroom and washed it off."

He held out the hand in question. Even in the darkly lit nightclub, Ava could see the smudged ink. She shrugged, secretly pleased that he'd washed off the hussy's phone number before coming to her.

Luke's hand grasped her waist and her heart skipped a beat as his heat seeped through the silk of her blouse. "If it hadn't been for that little pit stop, I would have been the one dancing with you instead of Pete and Griff," he growled. Ava felt her blood sing in her veins, all at once on fire and raging out of control.

Another slow song picked up where the other left off. They moved to the music. Ava let her mind drift in the sensual haze Luke weaved around them. After a few minutes, she became aware that he'd somehow maneuvered them down a long empty hallway, well away from everyone else. It was dark, shadowed, and not quite as loud in this part of the nightclub.

Luke tipped her head up, his blue-eyed heat all but demanding her undivided attention. "Come home with me, Ava. Let your guard down for just this once and come home with me."

"Because you've seen my legs, Luke?" She was desperate to scream 'yes!' The sickening truth of it was she'd follow him anywhere. But she was just woman enough to want to know which version of Ava Sweet he wanted. The tomboy animal lover or the skirt and strappy sandals version she'd created just for him. "You can see that I'm a flesh and blood woman so now I'm worthy of your attention? Is that it?"

Luke's hand tightened on her jaw and she winced. He loosened his fingers a fraction, but didn't let her go. "I told you on the phone I'd seen past the clothes a long time ago," Luke chastised. And then in a much softer tone, "My comments to Pete hurt you. I'm sorry, baby. But damn it all, I didn't want him thinking of you in a sexual way. I don't want *any* man thinking of you in that way. Only me. Don't let my big mouth ruin what we could have." His tone went as soft as velvet sliding over her skin. "We'll be good together. I know it in my bones. You know it too. Let me make you feel good."

He didn't wait for her answer. Luke's head swooped down as he took her mouth in a scorching show of possession and need.

Ava did the only thing she could in that space of time. She dug her hands into the luxurious softness of Luke McGiffin's hair and hung on for the ride. No matter the reason for Luke's sudden interest, she was being given a chance to make love to him. Ava wasn't one to look a gift horse in the mouth.

Luke felt Ava's surrender. It was all the encouragement he needed. Walking her backwards until he had her up against the cold brick wall of the nightclub, he pushed his tongue between her plump lips, savoring the sweet and sassy flavor of her. She moaned and vibrated against him. His body hardened. Luke planted his left hand on the wall next to her head while his right gripped her hips in a firm grasp, then he lowered himself enough so that the heavy weight of his cock was pressed against her soft pussy. He swore he could feel her pulsing heat clear through the layers of their clothing. His hips thrust forward and back several times. He wanted her to feel the entire length of him. She needed to get used to his body against hers. Christ, he wanted her! If they weren't in such a public place, he would've shoved up her tight little skirt and fucked her right there, amidst the loud music and wild crowd.

But he was still reeling from Ava's transformation. He didn't quite know how he felt about her new look. She was sex in heels. Hell, every guy in the bar had devoured her with his eyes the instant she walked through the door. Had he not been dancing with her, she would have had a score of men vying for her attention. The image didn't sit well with Luke. He wanted her all to himself. Still, his little butterfly had finally emerged from her cocoon. He'd damn well be the only man to capture and claim all that untamed beauty.

Luke lifted his head a mere breath away and growled, "Open your thighs, Ava."

She stood firm. Both of her strong, lean legs clenched together so tight a slip of paper wouldn't fit. He kissed his way down her neck and hummed his approval when his lips skimmed the upper swells of her breasts. He had the horrible suspicion that she was braless. The idea of her unfettered tits barely an inch from his hungry mouth was enough to set a blaze in the pit of his stomach.

"Please, baby," he begged, "open wider for me. I want to feel you." When Luke felt her legs shift apart, he wanted to soar to the moon.

He wedged a leg between her soft thighs and relished the gentle moans emanating from deep in her throat. Luke watched as her eyes drifted closed, her head lying against the wall. Her fingers tunneled their way through his hair seemingly of their own volition. As if attempting to pull him closer in her need for more.

Luke knew he could do anything he wanted in that moment. She wouldn't oppose him. It was a heady thought. Ava was always so damned headstrong. For her to submit to him so completely was intoxicating as hell.

Beyond denying either of them any longer, Luke pushed her tiny skirt higher up her thighs, very nearly exposing her panties. His larger body caged her in, ensuring a degree of privacy. When he was sure no other could see what he was doing, he allowed his eyes to be drawn downward. The tiniest glimpse of white lace was visible. His body raged with a lust he'd never before felt. God, he wanted to see her. All of her. No clothes, people, or dark shadows hindering his view. He wanted Ava's lovely curves on display for his pleasure alone.

Her hips thrust forward, moving back and forth against his throbbing erection. Luke had to clench his jaw to keep from groaning. She was so agitated and turned-on. His cock pressed hard against his jeans, desperate to get inside Ava's tight cunt.

Starving to touch her where she needed it most, Luke slid his fingers away from her hip and over to her burning sex. Her eyes flew open, wide and anxious. His gaze snared her, forcing her to watch as he slipped a finger beneath the elastic leg band, to the damp springy curls beneath.

"Luke, please, I..."

Ava's unfinished and breathless plea seemed torn from deep inside. Hearing his name uttered in such raw agony, had his dick dripping with pre-cum. Something inside him snapped.

"You're mine, Ava," he declared, as feelings of possession and desire welled up. "No other man has a right to touch you like this. This creamy pussy is for me to play with."

Then he slipped that single exploratory finger between her fleshy folds, relishing the way her body gripped him like a silken glove, pulling him deeper.

In one smooth stroke, Luke was buried clear to his knuckle inside Ava's creamy heat. "You're so fucking tight and wet, baby," he hissed, "I want my cock to feel this slippery little pussy."

"Yes, Luke!"

Hearing her passion mount was like nothing he'd ever experienced with any other woman. She was different. Flaming hot and untamed. Ava Sweet was every inch the stubborn, independent woman he'd come to ache for day in and day out. But she was also a woman with untapped passion.

Her body quivered as he swept his thumb back and forth over her clitoris. She clutched onto him in desperate need. One sexy leg came off the floor to wrap around his hips, her heel digging into his ass. He finger-fucked her with hard, fast thrusts. Merciless in his need to see her come. The instant Ava spun out of control, Luke felt it.

He dipped his head and covered her mouth, then plunged his finger deep one last time. She arched and screamed and Luke swallow the wild sounds whole. Her soft, tender tissues convulsed, tightening and throbbing with pleasure. As quick as a summer storm, Ava flew apart in his arms. He marveled at the sight of her. Luke couldn't wait to get her alone. To have his dick inside her when she let go the next time.

He'd thought of Ava Sweet. Fantasized about how satiny her skin might be beneath all her layers of cotton. Wondered at how quick she'd ignite once he got his hands filled with her tight little body. Now it was finally time for him to see for himself if his suspicions had been correct all along. He had figured Ava to be a livewire if she ever allowed her control to slip. Hell, judging by the way her fingers had been digging into his hair, pulling him forward for a deeper mating of lips and tongues, her body so eager and hot and voracious, he'd been right on the money. Luke was only too glad he was the recipient of all that hot passion.

He'd been ready to kick Pete's teeth in when he'd talked about Ava's body in such sexual terms. When he'd agreed to go out on the date, Luke had been ready to strangle the man. It was his own damn fault though. For some idiotic reason, Luke thought he'd have plenty of time with Ava. As if she would just sit around on her pretty little ass and wait on him to sow his wild oats.

Well, she'd stopped waiting. She was ready. The only question left unanswered was, how soon could he get her away from all the appreciative male scrutiny and back to his place?

Luke pulled his finger free and licked her tangy juices. She watched, her lips parted and eyes transfixed. "Tasty," he whispered against her ear. She licked her lips and stayed perfectly still as he smoothed her skirt down. Luke was way too delighted to hear an unhappy whimper from Ava as he pulled away. She tried to pull him back, but he wouldn't let her. It took all his strength of will to keep from giving into the little temptress. Her soft sighs and moans had his blood pounding so hard he could barely think straight as it was.

He let go of Ava long enough to unwind her fingers from his hair and clutch her wrists in one of his hands above her head. She opened her eyes then and stared at him. Her blue gaze so full of innocent wonder. Christ almighty, she was beautiful. Pete had said it exactly right. Ava didn't need makeup and fancy trappings. She was a natural beauty.

"I want you, baby," Luke growled. "Tell me we're on the same track here."

He watched her small pink tongue dart out and lick at her bottom lip. The small guileless action caused a shudder to roll through him.

"Yes, Luke," she replied huskily. "I want you. You have no idea how badly I've wanted you. If you deny me, I swear I'll die."

Luke said a silent prayer to the heavens above. He could have handled being run over by a Mack truck easier than he could have handled her rejection.

"Let's go."

Nothing more was said from either of them as they weaved their way through the nightclub. Luke scanned the crowd for Pete. Ready to battle over Ava if need by. Much to his consternation, Luke noticed him sitting at a table with his sister, Jen. Pete's arm was around her shoulders and the two were looking at each other as if they were... in love? Pete and Jen? He shook his head. That mess was for tomorrow. Tonight was for Ava. Nothing else mattered.

Forbidden Fruit: Chapter 4

Luke had never given his driving much thought before, but on the way to his house, he'd driven with the kind of speed and determination that would have made a NASCAR driver proud. Neither of them had said a word on the way home. And the silence only served to intensify the sparks jumping between them.

He swung his big silver truck in the garage and shut off the engine. She'd made a reference before about the size of his truck, as if he were over-compensating for the size of his dick. He'd merely winked at her and teased, "See for yourself, Dr. Doolittle." Ava, being Ava, had huffed and stalked off.

She wasn't saying a word now either. When he shoved the door open, coming around to her side to lift her out, she looked at him with a mixture of arousal and trust. With other women, he'd enjoyed the aroused look, but he'd shied away from the trust part. Coming from Ava, he liked both. He wouldn't mind seeing more of it actually. Crazy.

As he stepped through the door into the kitchen, Ava's arms came around his neck, holding onto him tight. Luke felt a shock of need run through him. He couldn't wait for the bedroom. He had to have a sample now. He put her down and pushed the door closed with his foot. She looked around, as if shy all of a sudden. He wasn't going to give her time to rethink her decision.

Luke began unbuckling his belt. "I want to see you suck me."

Her innocent eyes shot wide. "Here?"

"Mmm, right here. Get down on your knees, baby. Prove to me that this is what you want."

He drew his zipper down and watched her make up her mind. A million thoughts flitted over her face. He wasn't sure what she'd do. But as he pulled his fly open and took out his cock, Ava licked her lips. That little gesture had his tip weeping with joy. He knew the instant she made her decision, because a naughty smile played at the corners of her mouth. Ava hiked up her skirt and lowered herself to the floor. She looked up at him, her palms pressed against her thighs. Luke was a goner.

He stepped forward and growled, "Open wide." Ava eagerly obeyed. Very gently, Luke guided his thick length over her wet tongue. "Suck it good, baby."

Her hands wrapped around his length and took over, suckling the tip first then drawing him in further. Soon, he was buried deep inside her hot little mouth, his balls pressed against her chin. Luke grabbed a fistful of her hair and moved her head up and down his shaft, showing her how to please him. Her cheeks hollowed out and her tongue teased the slit in the end of his penis. As her fingers came up and cupped his sac, squeezing slightly, Luke hissed and pulled her off him. "That's enough. When I come, I want to be inside that pussy. Real deep. I want to fill you up, baby." He tucked himself back into his jeans, but left them undone, and then held out a hand. "Up we go. I've got plans for you tonight."

Ava placed her hand in his and let him pull her to her feet. "What sort of plans?" she asked a hint of fear in her voice.

Luke didn't answer. He simply turned her around and gave a little nudge towards his bedroom. Once inside, he issued another command. "Get on the bed, Ava."

She lay down on top of his brown plaid comforter, directly in the center. Still dressed. Perfect. He had her alone finally. No one to stand in the way of him and paradise. He took his time to look at her. Letting her stew in her own need. Luke wouldn't let her rush him. He'd never been allowed the luxury to stare at Ava and he was going to enjoy this moment. He'd always had to steal glances when she wasn't aware.

Not this time.

Luke flipped the switch on the lamp next to his bed, determined to see every inch of her. Ava fidgeted restlessly and his eyes were inexorably drawn to her cotton skirt. It was incredibly tight and stretchy, molding to her hips and belly like a second skin. Her pale-pink blouse had inched upwards, giving him little peeks of her ivory flesh. He'd never in his life found a bellybutton so sexy.

"Griff got at least one thing right tonight. You do look good enough to eat, Ava," Luke ground out, anxious to fill his hands and mouth with what was now *his.*

He put one knee on the bed and planted a hand beside her head then leaned down for a kiss. Her lips were so soft and smooth, like the skin of a ripe plum. As soon as their mouths touched, his body swelled more. It was instantaneous combustion. He desperately wanted to wrap himself around her, to slide so deep between her legs she could never squirm away from him again.

Luke lowered himself gently on top of her, his lips pressing warm kisses all over. Her soft cheeks. Her obstinate chin. He trailed a teasing path down her neck to her blouse. He stopped and looked at the filmy material and muttered, "This is very pretty, but I'm afraid it has to go." Then he started to undo the pearly buttons that ran down the center. One by one, Luke exposed her. When he reaching the last one, Luke swiftly popped it out of its safe little hole and spread the blouse open.

"Christ, Ava. What were you thinking?"

Ava frowned up at him, some of the dazed heat being

quickly replaced by confusion. "Huh?"

He touched one tiny, mauve-colored nipple. "No bra?"

She shrugged. "I never wear a bra. I'm not so big that it's noticeable."

Was she insane? "Ava, a man always notices. Trust me on this one." He thought of all the men at the club and wanted to howl at the moon. "I should bend you over my knee and spank your ass."

She squinted up at him, a mulish expression coming over her face. "You never noticed my lack of a bra."

"Didn't I?" Luke whispered, being deliberately vague. He dipped his head and sucked one hard peak into his mouth, taking in as much of her soft round flesh as he could. Ava moaned and went pliable beneath him. Luke took his time, going from one to the other, playing and licking Ava's supple little tits. Taking pleasure in the fact that he had her so eager and wanton. He bit at her nipple and she went up in flames, bucking and moaning his name. Luke lifted his head and surveyed his handy work. Her breasts were wet from his greedy mouth. Her nipples were so dark they reminded him of raspberries.

"You really are beautiful, baby, never doubt it." He took delight in the flush that covered her face and neck. Luke grabbed her hand in his and guided it to his aching shaft. "Feel what you do to me? Do you see how badly I want you?" Ava's small fingers slipped inside his opened fly and wrapped around his penis. She squeezed and Luke's body hummed at the sweet torment.

He halted her before things went too far. "Not yet. I want to try something first."

"What?"

She was breathless and aching for another orgasm. He could see it in the way her legs kept rubbing together. Her heart was pumping fast too. He could fuck her. Put them both out of their misery. But Luke wanted to make her squirm a little. To watch her plead for him to take her.

He left the bed, went to the closet, and chose two ties. When he came back, the silk dangling from his fingers, Ava's mouth dropped open in shock. "What are you going to do with those?"

"Tie your hands and blindfold you."

She blinked several times, and Luke had to give her credit for not leaping off the bed. Instinct told him she wasn't used to sexual games. Good. He liked knowing no other man had given her this sort of pleasure.

He aligned his body next to hers, propped himself up on his elbow and stared down at her. "Do you trust me enough to let me have my way with you, Ava?"

"I might not like it. I've never done this before, Luke."

Luke laid one tie on the bed. With the other, he teased her nipples, drifting the material over and around both breasts, then he glided it down her belly to her mound. She was still covered.

"Slip your panties off, but leave the skirt."

Ava quickly obeyed. She started to drop the small white cotton to the floor, but he was quick to grab them out of her hand. He brought them to his face and inhaled her womanly scent. "Mmm, such a sweet little pussy. And all mine."

"Oh."

The oval shape of her lips as she spoke sent him into overdrive. Luke dropped the panties onto his nightstand and went back to teasing her with the tie. He drifted the silk over her curls, then the soft, wet center of her. He flicked the end of the tie over her clit. Ava closed her eyes and arched upward, whimpering softly. Luke pulled the tie away and waited for her eyes to open again.

"I'm glad you've never done this, but there's no need to be scared. I won't do anything that you don't want."

Ava stared at him for so long, he thought she was going to tell him no. Her shy nod had his balls drawing up tight.

"Good girl," he praised, then he leaned down and kissed her. His tongue probed the seam of her lips and she parted, giving him access to the hot wet cavern. He flicked and sucked at her tongue, rewarding her for trusting him. When he pulled away, they were both panting. Her body scorched his everywhere their flesh touched. With great effort, Luke brought himself back to the game.

He rose to a sitting position then took one of her tiny wrists in his hand. She was so delicate. Ava had an inner strength that he admired, but when he held her fragile bones in his palm, Luke was reminded of how easily he could hurt her. He wrapped the tie around it once, then he did the same with her other wrist, before tying a knot in the center. It was loose, but that was the point.

"I can easily get free. It's not a very good knot, Luke."

He flicked the end of her impertinent nose. "That's the point. A good little girl will stay put. A bad girl will slip loose." Luke took the other tie and leaned in close. He nipped her earlobe, enjoying the way she moaned. "I wonder which you'll be."

"Depends."

The single word, spoken so low, caught him off guard. "On what?"

"What I get if I'm good and what happens if I'm bad."

Luke chuckled. "You sure caught on to the game quick, baby."

She grinned. "I'm a fast learner."

Luke covered her eyes with the tie, then instructed her to lift her head so he could tie it securely behind her head. "Does it feel okay?"

"Yes."

She was quiet and shy all of a sudden. Luke wasn't going to give her time to think too much. He left the bed and quickly stripped. Then went back and knelt between her thighs. Luke went straight for her sweet spot, grasping it between his index finger and thumb, he pinched lightly. Ava spread her legs wider, giving him permission to do more.

"If you're a good girl, you'll get to have my big cock inside your tight pussy and you'll get to come. A lot."

He sank two fingers inside her heat then, soaking them both with Ava's delicious juice. "But, if you're a bad girl, then I'll be forced to fuck your sweet little ass. And you'll have to ask my permission to come."

"Oh God."

He aligned his body along hers, keeping his fingers deep inside Ava, unmoving, and growled, "I wonder, are you a good little girl, Ava, or are you naughty?"

"Please, Luke."

She wiggled around beneath him, her hands tied together above her head. "Please what?"

"I can't wait any longer. Please, I need you inside of me."

"You'll have to wait."

She shook her head in denial. "No! Please fuck me. It feels as if I've waited for years to be here like this with you."

Luke warmed at her words. He kissed her gently and

then reared back to look at her disheveled clothing. Her shirt was flung open, her skirt pushed up around her waist. "You look like a little slut with that outfit all askew. I could fuck you so hard right now."

"Then do it!"

"This little pussy is hungry for me isn't it, Ava?" Luke growled, needing to hear her say it.

"Yes!" She screamed, the single word causing a maelstrom of need inside him. Luke felt crazed. Like a man gone mad.

"Give me time to play first," he whispered, then he pinched her tiny nub and Ava let out a moan. She pushed against his hand and abruptly Luke pulled away. "I want you on your hands and knees."

Ava hesitated, her pride stinging. Everything he'd done so far was beyond anything she'd ever experienced. She'd never known a more powerful man. He was pushing her beyond her comfort zone. Inadvertently, her body went stiff at his harsh command. She could see that he was content to let her take her time. He was so in control, while she was a wild mass of nerves and wants. It was frustrating.

Shocking him, Ava carefully turned onto her stomach. With her hands tied it wasn't easy, but she managed to get up on her hands and knees, the way he'd instructed. She left her pride behind and bared her soul, as well as her body. Her entire body shook with need.

"Jesus, you look good like this. I can see every detail of your sex and ass. I have to taste you, baby." Then he moved behind her and kissed her labia. "Mmm, perfect. All spicy and hot and slick."

At the first swipe of his tongue, her legs quivered, barely able to hold herself upright. He wrapped both his sinewy arms around each of her thighs and spread her open further. Luke plundered and explored her pussy. He was so gentle with her as he licked at her cleft, teasing a moan out of her. It wasn't enough. Ava wanted to feel his tongue probe deep. She had the sneaking feeling that it would never be enough with Luke. A lifetime spent making love, night and day would only whet her appetite. She wanted to please him. To tip him over that edge of desire. To hear his shout when he came.

The part of her brain still functioning couldn't believe she was doing this. She had the handsome, possessive Luke McGiffin between her thighs, licking and kissing and driving her wild. Ava planned to enjoy the hell out of every minute too.

When he took her tiny nub into his mouth and sucked at it, she lost control. Her thoughts were forgotten as he drew a long moan out of her. Feelings began to build and soon she was all but begging for release.

Ava pitched over the edge as he nibbled her clitoris. She lost all sense of time and place with the blindfold on. Inhibitions disappeared and she bucked against his face, her body turning to liquid lava.

"Oh, yes!" she shouted, then shattered into a million tiny shards.

Luke's assault didn't end there. He continued to tease her clit, causing her to squirm. Evidently, he wasn't satisfied with her pleading, because he used his fingers on her as well, inserting one at first, then two. Barely edging his way in, he expertly wiggled them back and forth. The dual sensation of his mouth sucking at her, and his fingers stroking at the sensitive nerve endings just inside her cleft, tore a scream from her. "Luke, I can't!"

"You can," he hissed against her flesh, then flicked one more time. Ava flew high, higher than ever, over some invisible edge. From far off in the distance, she heard Luke's soft words of approval.

"That's it baby, let it go. I've got you," he soothed.

And he did, she realized. His arms were wrapped so tightly around her upper thighs that it was a wonder she could feel her legs at all.

Ava felt Luke kiss her mound, then pull away. But just as quickly, he was back. With his cock at her entrance, his hands wrapped around her hips, he held her still.

"You've been a very good girl, Ava. But someday, soon, I'm going to have to fuck this pretty ass."

Then he slowly pushed into her, just barely

breaching her entrance, before pulling all the way out again. Ava whimpered, wanting, needing him to fill her. She felt his knee nudging her legs wider. She was so ready for him, so swollen and dripping wet. His cock slid deep and she screamed his name. He was so big. Her very limited experience hadn't adequately prepared her for his girth.

"Damn, Ava, you feel so good. So tight and hot I'm burning up for you, baby."

His words fueled her libido further. He took his time, finding the right rhythm. Her body clenched the further in he went.

"Don't go rigid on me, Ava."

"I... I can't help it, Luke. It's just so perfect." Tears sprang to her eyes and she closed her lids in a lame attempt to keep them to herself. "You can't know how badly I've wanted this."

He leaned down and kissed his way up her spine. Her heart shuddered in her chest. "Yeah, we're perfect together. Remember that." And then he plunged deep, burying himself completely.

Ava arched her back and pushed against him, moving her hips in little circles, increasing their pleasure. His control seemed to snap like a frayed fishing line.

Luke's body came down against hers as he planted his hands on the mattress beside her, caging her in and holding her still for his loving. He moved in and out, fucking her. She knew, even with the blindfold, that he was watching every move and listening to every sound she made. As her passion mounted again, his gentle thrusts became harder, faster. His balls slapped her clit with each inward stroke. She felt a warm hand palming her right breast. Luke's tongue drifted back and forth over her shoulder, then his teeth nibbled at the tendon. He sucked and teased, while his hips drove into her. Over and over again, until Ava flung her head back and shouted out his name. Her climax built and built. Inner muscles squeezed his dick tight. His body slammed into hers one last time, and then he was filling her with his hot seed.

They both collapsed onto the bed, Luke on top of her limp body. She didn't care. Having Luke on top made her feel safe, loved even. Strong fingers pulled off her blindfold, then untied her hands. She squeezed her eyes shut to the brightness of the room.

"You are a surprise, Ava Sweet. An amazing, sexy, surprise."

She didn't know what to say to that, so she stayed quiet. He kissed her cheek, then pulled his cock free and left the bed—to dispose of the condom she assumed. When he came back, she was half-asleep already. Had it not been for his next words, she would have drifted into a cozy little REM state.

"Tomorrow, we'll talk."

And so, Ava's pleasure bubble popped.

"There it's gone. But the next time you have a rat or a *field mouse*," she said, rolling her eyes, "you don't need to call me, just get a cat and let nature take its course."

Luke scowled, looking all the more adorable for it. "Look, I could give a flying fuck about the mouse. I wanted to see you, Ava."

Her stomach bottomed out. Here it comes. The big let down. Luke was already regretting their night together. This was exactly what she'd been trying to avoid.

In an effort to dodge the uncomfortable morning after discussion, she'd slipped out of his bed and walked barefoot the few blocks back to her house in the wee hours of the morning. She'd used that time to give into a good long cry too. Now it was Sunday afternoon and she was forced to face him again. Life was too cruel sometimes.

"Well, here I am."

Luke crossed the room so they were only inches apart. "Why'd you leave me, baby? I've been going crazy. You wouldn't return my phone calls. I stopped by your place half dozen times yesterday and you refused to answer the door. If it hadn't been for the mouse, you'd still be avoiding me."

She sighed. "We're no good together. Friday night was a mistake, Luke, you and I both know it." She started to back her way towards the door. "Let's just forget it ever happened."

Luke's eyes roamed over her body, igniting her on fire with the heat in his gaze. "I'll never forget the way you looked in my bed. And I sure as hell won't forget how pretty you are when you come."

Ava threw her hands in the air and yelled, "Why are you doing this?"

Luke closed the distance between them and took her into his arms, then kissed her senseless. His warm lips coaxed hers to open. Ava was helpless to deny him. The instant she parted, he was there, teasing and setting off a million different feelings at once. His hand fisted in her hair and he pulled her head back for better access. Her body arched against his and she felt the unmistakable evidence of his arousal. Knowing where he was headed, Ava pushed against his chest and yanked out of his arms.

She was panting and on edge when she demanded, "Look at me, Luke. Really look. These jeans and t-shirt, this is the real me. This is who I am."

He looked. His eyes a possessive brand as they journeyed from her tennis shoes to her plain white t-shirt. "You look sweet and innocent and so hot I'm ready to push you against the door and fuck you until you moan my name."

Ava groaned and dropped her head into her hands. "Oh, God."

A moment or two later, she felt strong fingers beneath her chin, coaxing her to lift her head. When she did, it was to see Luke holding a puppy. *A puppy?* She reached out and stroked. It was the cutest little black and white puppy she'd ever seen.

"Oh, aren't you just so adorable!" Ava murmured, her anger disappearing in an instant, completely enchanted with the tiny bundle of joy. "Where'd you come from, Oreo?"

Luke's brow shot up. "You've given her a name already?"

Ava blinked. "Sorry. She just looks like an Oreo, I guess."

He smiled and ruffled Oreo's fur. An odd sensation unfurled in Ava's belly. Both of the things she loved with all her heart were right in front of her. It all became too much. Ava covered her face and did something she'd vowed to never do in the presence of Luke McGiffin.

She cried.

Luke sat the puppy on the floor. Within seconds she was curled up on the end of the couch, snoring. Taking Ava's chin in his hand, Luke forced her to look at him. "Does this mean you don't like the present, baby?" he asked gently.

"Present?"

Luke smiled. "I bought her for you, Dr. Doolittle."

Ava's heart squeezed, he was calling her Doolittle again. Was the puppy a consolation prize then?

"You bought her for me? Is this like one of those, 'the sex was grand, but once was enough', kind of presents?"

"No, baby, nothing like that." He touched the tip of her nose. "I wanted to get you something and I knew she would be perfect the instant I saw her. There is one condition though."

Her eyes narrowed. "And just what might that be?"

"I come with her. We're a package deal."

Her mouth dropped open. Surely she hadn't heard him right. "You and Oreo? You both want to be... *mine*?"

Luke leaned forward and kissed her. It was soft and fleeting. Darn it, Ava really wanted more. A lot more. She'd never get enough of his kisses.

"I love you, Ava. I want to be yours."

"What about your other girlfriends?" she needed it all on the table. "You like having your freedom. You've said it more than once."

"I've wanted you for awhile now, Ava. If you'd been paying attention, you would have noticed my lack of a social life for the past six months." And as if that wasn't enough of a bomb, he dropped one more on her, just for good measure. "I even gave my little black book away."

Ava rubbed her eyes. Scared and overwhelmed at once.

"Well?" he asked. "Don't you have anything to say?"

He sounded so disgruntled, maybe even a little bit scared. Could it really be true? "You love me, Luke?" Before he could answer, she went for broke. "Because I've loved you forever. Once I have you, I won't be taking you back for a refund either. All sales are final."

He grinned lasciviously at her. "Sold." Then his expression turned intense as he murmured, "Now, I want you naked and in my bed."

Ava grinned. "Yeah, that works for me," because then he'd be naked too.

Luke reached around her and swatted her bottom. "Get moving," he growled. "I've waited over twenty-four hours to have you back in my arms. A man has only so much patience, baby."

Ava laughed and ran for the bedroom, Luke hot on her heels. As soon as she entered, he started yanking at his clothes. She helplessly followed suit, captivated as he unwrapped his gorgeous body. The moment they were both naked, he pushed her onto the mattress and covered her with his body. "You drive me wild, Dr. Doolittle," he hissed, then he touched and stroked. Ava was about to pull him down for a kiss, but he stopped her with a finger to her lips.

"You were a very bad girl, leaving me that way. Remember what I said happens to bad girls, baby?"

"Oh my."

Luke winked. "Turn over; it's time to take your punishment."

Ava hesitated. "I'm not sure about this, Luke."

"Never had a man inside that sexy ass of yours?" She shook her head. "Good. That means its uncharted territory."

She would have laughed had she not been so nervous. "Maybe it should stay uncharted."

"Nope. It needs to be explored. Thoroughly."

"How about next time," she hedged.

Luke made a tsking sound. "You should know by now that I wouldn't do anything to cause you pain. Give it a chance, baby. If you don't like it, we'll stop. I promise."

She still didn't think this was something she was going to like, but she trusted Luke. Ava turned over. Luke reached over and grabbed something off the nightstand. She frowned when she saw what it was.

"Warming lubricant?"

Luke grinned down at her. "I planned ahead. The instant I found you gone, I went shopping. Oreo wasn't the only thing I bought for you today."

He drizzled the oil onto her buttocks and began massaging the liquid into her flesh. Her skin heated instantly. When she felt his fingers dip into her seam and probe her anus, Ava moaned.

The rest of the day was spent with Luke teasing and toying with her body, touching her in the most taboo of places. She had three orgasms before he finally allowed himself to come. Afterwards, he'd taken her to his shower where he spent a great amount of time washing every inch of her body.

Ava reveled in it because in that moment she knew the truth. All that mattered was that Luke loved her. He was the only man with the power to stir her passion in ten seconds flat. To Ava, it was only more proof that they were a perfect fit. Oh, yeah, life with bad boy Luke McGiffin would be one very wild ride.

Later in the evening, as they ate pizza and watched an old John Wayne western, Oreo sleeping soundly in her lap, Jen called. She wanted to let them both know that she and Pete were planning a trip to the Amish country in Northern Ohio. Luke went into big brother mode instantly, demanding that Pete stay away from his sweet, innocent baby sister.

But with a few strategically placed kisses, Ava managed to bring him away from thoughts of bodily harm and onto more pleasant things. Like what it's like to be at the mercy of one Dr. Doolittle. Being a good sport, Luke didn't complain one bit when she insisted on riding him, while he lay tied and blindfolded this time, totally at her mercy.

Afterwards, they both fell into a deep sleep. Monday came way too early.

Epilogue

"A double wedding?" Luke asked.

Ava and Luke were sharing a booth at their favorite pizza parlor with Jen and Pete. It'd been three months since the big makeover. She'd since moved into his house and had sold hers. Luke was adjusting well to everything, with the exception of Pete and Jen's relationship. He was still concerned about Pete taking advantage of his *innocent* sister. If he only had a clue.

"I think it sounds like a great idea,' Pete chimed in. "And it'll be cheaper."

Jen frowned. "Cheaper?"

Pete paled. "Not cheaper, but more... cost efficient. The extra money could go towards new furniture for the house." Jen's frown worsened. "And think of all the fun you and Ava will have planning it together!"

Jen's expression lightened a degree. "It would be a lot of fun." she aimed a smile at Luke. "What do you say, big brother?"

Luke pulled Ava in closer to his side and announced, "It's up to Ava. If she wants a double wedding, then that's what she'll get."

"Sharing the biggest day of my life with my two best friends? Definitely a great idea."

Pete leaned over and kissed Jen. Luke cleared his throat, causing Jen to pull away and Pete to grin mischievously. Ava decided now was as good a time as any to share her big news. She'd been looking for the right opportunity and this seemed to be it.

"I have an announcement to make."

"You're quitting your job?"

That threw her for a loop. "Why would you think that?"

"Wishful thinking," Luke growled. "I don't like you working for that asshole. Every damn time Dr. Ryan is near you, he comes onto you."

Ava rolled her eyes. "I can take care of myself. Besides, in a few more months it won't be an issue."

"He's got a boner for you, baby, a few months won't make a damn bit of difference."

She ignored Luke's warning and confessed, "I'm pregnant."

Luke choked on his soda. Jen screamed and began bombarding her with questions. Pete had gotten up to smack Luke on the back. Ava wasn't sure if it was to help him breathe or comfort him in his time of need.

After the initial shock wore off the table fell silent. Luke stared at her belly, as if he were trying to see right through to her womb for confirmation. Finally he spoke.

"How far along are you?"

Ava wasn't sure what to think of his attitude. He was

so still and quiet. "Just eight weeks."

"You've been to a doctor?" She nodded. "The baby's... healthy?" She nodded again. "I'm going to be a father," he conceded. Finally, Ava found her voice.

"And I'm going to be a mother. We'll make good parents. Don't you think?"

Luke pulled her across the seat and kissed her. His mouth, hard and demanding. Ava moaned and wrapped her arms around his neck and sank everything she had into the kiss. His tongue licked her lower lip, and then sucked it into his mouth. When she felt his hands coasting over her back, just barely grazing the top of her jeans, she remembered where they were.

Ava broke the kiss, both of them panting and breathless. Pete whistled low. Jen giggled. Luke was the first to speak.

"I love you and I love that you're having my baby. I can't wait to make an honest woman of you. Very soon you'll be Mrs. Luke McGiffin."

"So you're okay with the pregnancy? I mean, I know it's unexpected and sort of out of order since we're not married yet."

He stroked a calloused hand over her cheek and murmured, "I'm thrilled. Never doubt it." He placed his palm protectively over her abdomen. "I can't believe my baby is in there. It's amazing."

Ava laughed and placed her own hand over his. Jen squealed. "I'm going to be an Aunt! Oh my lord, I'm going to spoil that kid rotten."

They all tipped up their sodas, toasting the miracle of life. Ava silently thanked the fates for giving her so much to be grateful for.

Eh, she'd give it a few days before telling him what else the Doctor had discovered when he'd done the ultrasound. After all, a woman had to be very particular when she told her husband-to-be that they were about to have triplets.

Reckless

Exposure

To My Reader:

Bad boys from the wrong side of the tracks and small town good girls, there's nothing sexier! Rand and Lucy are so different it's crazy. Of course they belong together. I hope their erotic tale makes you sweat!

-Anne Rainey

Reckless Exposure: Prologue

Rand had one rule. Never get involved with a model. For five years that rule had stayed unbroken. But this dark-haired beauty with the innocent eyes and sweet smile did things to him, wicked things. He groaned as she posed for his camera. There were times when rules needed to be tossed, and this was one of those times. Later he'd probably kick his own ass, but for now all that mattered was spending more time with Lucy Flemming.

A newbie in the business, Lucy could easily end up devoured by the many vultures that inhabited the fashion world. Hell, they could chew her up and spit her out within weeks. Rand had a feeling about Lucy, though. She possessed a quality that would push her right to the top. It wasn't just her naivety, her naughty girl grin or her killer legs. It was the intelligence in her eyes. There was more to Lucy Flemming than a pretty face, and that was something every modeling agency craved.

After Rand snapped the last shots and put the camera down, Lucy let out a long breath, as if she'd found the entire session difficult. Why would a woman so unused to modeling be in *his* studio? He had a reputation as one of the best fashion photographers in New York. He took on professionals, not little girls from Zanesville, Ohio.

Lucy pulled the ruby-red robe he'd laid out for her over her alabaster shoulders. Rand found himself stepping closer, his curiosity getting the better of him. "So, George told me you wanted to get into modeling. I usually don't photograph newbies, but for George I made an exception."

Lucy smiled and Rand's gut clenched. Jesus H, she was a beauty. The real thing, too, not some product of a surgeon's knife. After five years of staring at women through a camera lens, he could easily spot the surgically enhanced from the naturals. Lucy was a gift straight from heaven.

"Thanks. I really appreciate you seeing me on such short notice." She tied the robe closed, hiding the bikini she wore. "I know about your reputation, Mr. Miller, and I'm grateful you took the time to see me tonight."

"How do you know George, anyway? He's not exactly a sociable guy." That was putting it mildly. The millionaire fashion designer had all of two friends and they were both of the canine variety.

"Ah, now that's a funny story."

"I'm all ears." And he was. She had his full attention. God, she was breathtaking. Her genuine laughter felt like sunshine on a cold winter day. And the habit she had of biting her lower lip was fucking adorable.

"George knew my mother."

It shocked him that the arrogant, aloof George could know anyone on a personal level. "Really?"

"Yep. A few years ago, they were in the same hospital together. My mother went in for gall bladder surgery, George was there for—well, maybe I shouldn't say. It's probably private."

Rand winked. "I promise not to tell." He led her into the kitchen, grabbed a bottle of water from the fridge for each of them, and handed her one. She took it and chugged down half the contents.

His attention was so focused on the way her little pink tongue swiped at her lower lip that he lost track of what she'd said. "I'm sorry, what?"

"Colon surgery," she repeated. "He went in to have some polyps removed."

Rand had to fight to control his laughter. The stick up George's ass must have been a little too much for him to handle.

Lucy placed the bottle on the counter that separated his studio from the kitchen area and sat on one of the stools. "I still don't know how it started, but when I came to pick up mom, I met George. He'd been talking to my mother for a while. I think he was a little enamored of her. Mom tends to have that effect on men. Anyway, before he left he gave me his card and told me if I was ever in New York and needed anything I should give him a call." She stretched her arms. "And here I am."

Something about her story didn't add up. He stepped closer and propped an elbow on the counter. "George never leaves New York, ever. So how could your mother and George end up in the same hospital?"

Lucy slid her bottled water back and forth on the counter. "But George was in Ohio. His brother is a doctor there. He referred him to the surgeon who did the deed."

That shocked him. "George has a brother?"

Lucy laughed. "You sound so surprised. Did you think he was hatched in a lab or something?"

"That would be more believable." Rand shook his head. "I had no idea George had any family at all, much less a brother. Just goes to show how well you know people, huh?"

She twirled the bottle and murmured, "I guess."

His hands itched to touch her. To untie the robe and feel the satiny skin of her belly against his fingers and lips. Rand cleared his throat and asked, "So, are you doing anything after this?"

Lucy looked at the clock on the far wall. "It's ten o'clock at night. What's there to do besides go home and climb into bed?"

He leaned across the countertop and whispered, "You're in New York. This is the city that never sleeps, remember?"

She leaned back, a subtle feminine retreat. Between

her fast breathing and the way she kept biting that tempting lower lip, Rand recognized the signs of arousal. She might be hesitant, but she was still intrigued.

"Don't remind me. I don't think I've slept since I got here. The noise in my apartment building never stops."

"You've been in New York how long?"

"A little over a month. I'm hoping to make some extra cash modeling so I can pay for college. I want to get into fashion design."

"I know it's rude, but how old are you?"

Lucy seemed to cringe at his question. "I'm twenty-two. I know, I know, I'm way too old to consider a real modeling career, but I have no intention of doing it after I finish college."

Thank God. Rand had started to wonder if she was underage. She could be lying, but Lucy didn't strike him as the type. Hell, at thirty years old Rand knew he had no business going anywhere near the innocent Lucy Flemming, but short of being run over by a bus, nothing was going to keep him from her. "You don't look twenty-two. You look younger, and that's all that matters in this line of work."

"Thanks."

He had to tamp down the urge to touch her, to taste her. A few inches closer and he'd be able to see for himself if her glistening lips were as delicious as they looked. He stepped back and forced himself to take it slow. "Want to go somewhere and grab a burger?"

She propped her hand on her hip. "Are you trying to fatten me up?"

He tossed his empty water bottle in the recycling bin. "Go to the gym tomorrow and work it off. I promise it'll be worth every ounce of sweat."

"Throw in a beer and I'm there."

Damn, he loved the way her mind worked. "Deal."

She got off the stool and started toward the dressing room. "Just give me five minutes!"

Rand watched her walk away, her heart-shaped ass beckoning him beneath the red satin. Christ, he wanted her. No way in hell was he letting her get away. Lucy Flemming had just been claimed. She just didn't know it yet.

Reckless Exposure: Chapter 1

Two Months Later

"Thanks for taking me to the movies. I know romantic comedies aren't your thing, but I really had fun."

"They're usually not my thing, but I actually liked it. Don't tell anyone, though. I'd lose my manly-man badge."

Lucy laughed. "Your secret is safe with me."

Rand held the door to the cab for her, slid in beside her, and gave the cabbie his address. Then he turned to her. "Good. Now, back to us."

His softly whispered words slipped down her spine in a gentle caress. "Us?"

"Yeah. It's been two months since we first met."

"Yes."

He placed his hand on her thigh and caressed her. She could barely see his midnight-blue eyes in the dark confines of the cab. His shaggy sandy-blonde hair and muscled torso had her body spinning out of control. He was incredibly rugged and so very male. Her pussy flooded with heat every single time she looked at him.

"I care about you, Lucy. More than any woman I've ever known."

Her heartbeat accelerated. "It's the same for me."

He leaned toward her and Lucy's flesh heated up at his nearness. When his lips were mere inches from hers, he murmured, "I want you. I wanted to give you some space, I swear I did, but that just doesn't seem to be the smart thing to do anymore."

It was now or never. In the two months she'd dated the wild man, he'd shown her things she'd never known existed. In her heart she knew he was way out of her league. He lived on the edge, always pushing the limits. When he wasn't careening down the highway on his Harley, he was skydiving off some jagged cliff in Taupo, New Zealand. He was so worldly, and she was just a girl from Ohio. She'd never understood what he saw in her. But questioning it to death had gotten her exactly nowhere. It was time to act like a woman, not a child.

"I think the only smart thing to do is kiss me," she murmured.

"Mmm, yeah, good idea." He groaned, and then his lips covered hers.

Lucy melted. He was so tender, so warm, and she badly wanted it to last forever. As his tongue coasted over her lips, she let out a sigh and parted for him. He took his time, dipping and tasting her as if he had all the time in the world. She wrapped her arms around his neck and pulled him in deeper, edgy all at once for everything. He groaned and suddenly his warm palm was against her bare midriff beneath her tank, inching upwards until the caress of his thumb had her breast vibrating with need. When she whimpered, Rand lifted his head, his gaze zeroing in on the cabbie. Lucy flushed with embarrassment. She'd all but forgotten they weren't alone.

With both of them trying to catch their breath, Rand was the first to recover. "I think we've gone as far as we can without being arrested," he whispered for her ears alone.

Her cheeks heated over her hedonistic reaction to a simple kiss. She sat away and smoothed down her tank with shaky fingers. "I think maybe you're right. I should get home, anyway."

Strong fingers cupped her chin and coaxed her gaze back to his. "Home with me or home alone?"

This was it. Her chance to back out. That he was even willing to give her an out made her decision easier. Instinctively Lucy knew he would never hold it against her if she left him hard and aching. The first night they'd gone out, they'd both gotten carried away, but he'd backed off as if content to let her come to him. For two months he'd been sweet and patient. Now she didn't want him to be either of those things. She craved him in a way she'd never craved a man.

"Home with you," she answered as a new determination filled her with strength.

Rand leaned over and branded her lips with his possessive heat. Neither of them spoke for the rest of the drive. Her nerves fairly vibrated with the energy pulsing through her veins, and her mind reeled at what she was about to do. She knew by the way he clenched his fists that he was just as wildly turned on, which gave her the power to shove her last few worries away.

Within minutes they were cocooned in the privacy of his apartment. She'd had sex with all of two men and neither of those experiences were anything to brag about. Anxiety welled up and threatened to consume her. Damn, she might as well be a scared teenager for all the experience she possessed. Rand didn't appear to have the same reservations. The passion in his gorgeous blue eyes was all the evidence she required.

"I want you, baby," he said, "real bad." He turned the lock on the front door and moved toward her. "But I need to know you won't regret a single minute of this. Tell me." Rand paused inches away from her. "I want to hear it from your lips."

Hearing him say it and seeing the raw ache etched into his harsh features effectively caused her own daring confidence to surface.

"I do want you, Rand," she softly confirmed, staring up at him, allowing the uneasiness to show on her face. "But I haven't had a lot of lovers. I'm a little nervous."

He closed the space between them and took her into the warm, solid comfort of his arms. "Don't be afraid of me, Lucy. I'd never hurt you."

He brushed his lips across the top of her head. The gentleness of his touch stirred her clear to her toes.

"We'll take it real slow. All you have to say is stop, and we stop. You have my word on that."

She felt childish in the face of his confidence. "The very last thing I want is for you to stop."

It was way past time for a man like Rand to come into her life and teach her how to feel like a woman. She wanted his touch, his all-consuming desire. She was no fool. She knew their relationship was probably temporary. She feared she had already fallen in love with Rand, but that didn't mean he felt the same way about her. Did she want to waste another minute worrying over it tonight? No, all that mattered in that moment, all she craved was to feel him sinking inside her, filling her, bringing her to the very brink of ecstasy and beyond.

Pushing her fears aside, she stepped out of his arms, gripped the hem of her tank and yanked it over her head. She dropped it to the floor and stood perfectly still, resisting the urge to cringe and cover herself while his dark gaze roamed greedily over her torso. It hadn't been the first time he'd seen her breasts, but it was the first time she'd taken the initial step.

Her nipples hardened as the cool air hit her and she shivered. She'd gone without a bra because she hadn't intended to do anything more than work on her finances, until Rand showed up at her apartment insisting they celebrate their two-month anniversary. Now Lucy was grateful she didn't have to gracefully and seductively wrestle with straps and hooks. And the heated look in her lover's eyes was enough to set her insides fluttering.

"Damn." Rand couldn't move or even breathe. She was perfect. His dream woman and then some. Her breasts were like large, soft, round pillows of creamy flesh. Christ, he could get lost for a decade playing with Lucy's bountiful swells. He ached to taste her rosy nipples. Lick and bite and suck until his heart was content.

His hand reached out of its own volition and stroked one turgid peak. Her breathing hitched and she arched into his palm. He lost it. Stepping forward, he wrapped an arm around her lower back and drew her against his chest, pressing and flattening her pretty tits against his t-shirt, driving himself crazy with the feel of her as he took her mouth. At the sweet flavor of her lips, his sense of calm scattered.

He drank in her moan of excitement and licked at her full lower lip. He'd never get enough of her taste. He invariably went to bed thinking of her. He woke tormented by the hottest dreams he'd ever experienced. Holding back, waiting for the right moment hadn't been easy, but it had been worth it. Since the instant she strolled into his studio, she'd been his temptation.

Like a gentle lamb teasing the big nasty wolf. Now she was here, in his arms, clutching at him with eager abandonment. She trusted him with something special. The thought gave him a possessive kind of pleasure, even while a trickle of fear rose up. He didn't want to disappoint her. He wanted to give her nothing but pleasure. Satisfy her every which way he could. Bring her to the very brink of orgasm before pulling back and doing it all over again until she begged for release. He'd touched her several times over the last two months. He'd sunk his fingers into her tight little pussy and he'd wrung cries of need from her. Now, knowing just how tight she'd be when his cock stretched and filled her made him swell painfully hard.

"Open those sweet lips for me, baby," he groaned against her mouth.

She did as he commanded. Rand took the advantage and slipped into the wet warmth, tasting and swirling his tongue over and around hers, sipping at her with a kind of crazy fever that went beyond anything he'd ever experienced. When she whimpered and drew her arms around his neck, he felt the last thread on his control snap.

Keeping his lips firmly against hers, he bent and hooked his arm behind her knees, then lifted her into his arms, cradling her nude torso close. He wanted her completely bare. He wanted to see all of her. From head to toe, so he could work his tongue over her, inch by slow, delectable inch.

As Rand laid her out on the comforter and broke the kiss, he got his first glimpse of Lucy's eyes. The light brown shade he'd drowned in countless times had darkened to almost the shade of milk chocolate. He could so easily drown in their mysterious depths. His jaw locked. He yearned to rip her shorts and panties down her legs and take her. Hard. Fast. Toss caution to the wind.

He shoved a hand through his hair and made one last attempt to take it slow, to make it good for Lucy. She was giving herself to him and he would cherish that if it killed him. He wanted to show her every kind of delicious pleasure imaginable. To addict her to him so she'd come back tomorrow night and the night after that. He never wanted to let her go. If he took her like a wild animal, she'd be disappointed or disillusioned. He would rather die than hurt Lucy. The notion took his ardor down a notch. Barely.

He watched her lick her lips and shift restlessly on the bed. Her nipples drew into tight hard peaks, begging to be nibbled on. Her long dark hair, the stuff of fantasies, spread out all around her, tucked beneath and partially covering her at the same time. Rand loved looking at her, but he was going to enjoy touching her even more.

He grasped the edges of his t-shirt and pulled it off. Then he moved to the waistband of his jeans, thrilled at the eager way Lucy licked her lips and stared in wide-eyed readiness at his fly.

Before he gave in to her silent pleas, he softly demanded, "Take off your shorts and panties for me, Lucy. Slowly. One at a time. So I can watch every inch you expose."

She stiffened and he feared she was going to balk at the idea of stripping for him. He'd taken countless pictures of her since their first photo session, but she still shied away from her own nudity. Finally, she slipped a single finger beneath either side of her drawstring shorts and tugged. She wiggled her hips and the shorts slithered downward, exposing a pair of cotton bikini panties with red hearts all over them. When she had the shorts down around her ankles, she kicked her foot outward and they flung to the floor.

"Christ, Lucy, you're so fucking sexy. I'm dying just looking at you." His muscles tightened as he stood frozen, staring. He understood beauty. After all, it was his business to know how to get the money shots. Great lighting, the best cameras, and lots of experience. But Lucy tore him up. It was as if he'd been waiting his entire life for this one moment.

"Now you, Rand." Her words feathered over him, effectively bringing him out of his hypnotic stupor.

"The panties first, Lucy. Take them off for me. Let me see that pretty pussy, baby."

Her chest rose and fell with her rapid breaths. The

little telltale sign proved to him that Lucy liked his little game. She was nervous, but turned on. He couldn't seem to help himself. It drove him wild to watch her capitulate to his orders.

She slipped her slender fingers beneath the elastic band of her panties and slid them down and off her long shapely legs. After waiting for what seemed an eternity, Rand got his first glimpse of Lucy's dark brown curls. She'd let him touch her, but always in the dark. As his gaze devoured her smooth creamy skin against his black comforter in the soft light from the table, he knew the wait had been well worth it.

Within a heartbeat he was free of his jeans and underwear and on the bed beside Lucy. Surely he'd died and gone to heaven. It was as simple as that.

Lying propped up on his elbow, he stayed silent as he watched her wide-eyed gaze wander over him. He wanted to grab her, slam her down on his heavy erection and pump her full. Time, he told himself. She needed time to get used to him first. To do that she would have to drop her shyness. He could tell she was still holding herself in check, uncertain. But he wanted to prove to her she could trust in him to give her pleasure and gentleness both, not just a quick fuck. First, he wanted her to open up a little. To face up to her desires.

"Do you like what you see?" he asked, his voice a hoarse whisper of sound in the quiet room.

Her gaze darted to his and she promptly nodded.

"Uh-uh," he chastised. "Not good enough. Tell me what your body wants, baby. Be honest with me."

He stroked a finger over her arm as her throat worked, as if mustering the courage. In a bare whisper she answered, "Yes, Rand, I want you. I want everything from you."

As her words sank in, his body vibrated. Fire licked at his insides. "I'm glad, Lucy, very glad."

He lowered his head to her breasts and took one tempting nipple into his mouth, suckling and tonguing her with greedy delight. She gasped and arched helplessly against him. He slid his arm beneath her back and lifted her, pressing her heavy breasts against his face while he toyed with the hard raspberry tip. When she cried out his name, he lifted away and began to tease her other delicious tit with the same avid attention. Her fingers sifted through his hair and her lower body squirmed with little shocks of pleasure. She was close. Already so eager to come. He could feel the rising passion in the way her heartbeat sped up and her fingers tightened. Not yet. He wanted her mindless with it. Craving him the way he craved her.

He released her nipple and kissed the delicate bud before lifting his head. "You want more?"

"Please, don't stop."

He let his hand drift down her body, bypassing her pussy, before smoothing his palm over her thigh. "Tell me what you want from me, Lucy. Don't be shy, not with me."

"I-I don't think I can. Please, Rand."

It was beautiful to watch her squirm restlessly atop the bed for him, so hungry and wild.

"Please what? Please suck you some more?" The intense blaze heating his blood grew hotter and hotter.

"Yes!"

"Where would you like my mouth, baby?" he said, feigning innocence. "Your beautiful tits?" He pinched one turgid peak, then the other, the little touches eliciting another moan from his sweet Lucy.

"Or would you rather I suck you right *here*?" he asked as he let his finger travel a scorching path down her belly to her dark ringlets.

Lucy grabbed his hand and clutched it against her mound. "Everywhere. I need you so bad it hurts."

"Mmm, let me see if I can't change that pain to pleasure," he murmured, and then he drifted his way down her body, leaving tiny kisses along the sides of her breasts and her ribcage. Her belly button got extra attention. She had the cutest belly button he'd ever seen. He wanted it pierced so he could play with the little jewel with his tongue. Groaning as he came to the notch between her legs, he inhaled deeply, taking her tangy scent inside his body for all time.

"Damn, woman, you take my breath away." It was the last thing he uttered before he spread her legs wide and tasted her.

He placed his lips against her clit and kissed the swollen and sensitive bit of flesh. A primitive growl reverberated inside his chest at the way her body began to move against his face. When he parted her with his fingers and sank his tongue deep into her hot opening, Lucy practically thrust him right off the bed.

Christ, she was so fucking responsive. The sudden burning thought of another man doing this to her had him nearly snarling. Rand had never felt such a powerful mix of tenderness and possessiveness for a woman. He wasn't sure he liked it one damn bit, either.

Aching to claim and mark her in some elemental way, he began sliding his tongue in and out of her, slowly, building her pleasure by small degrees, and then he used his thumb to stroke over her soft clitoris. He licked and nibbled, plying her flesh until all too quickly she screamed his name and buried her fingers in his hair, anchoring him to her as she rode out a wild and glorious climax.

As she slowly floated back down, Rand lifted himself off the bed and moved to his dresser to get a condom. No way could he take another minute of being this close to paradise without wanting to bury himself balls deep.

Lucy shifted on the bed. He turned and saw her staring at him. *Oh, hell.* He grabbed a handful of the packets. No way would one be enough. He went back to stand beside the bed, smiling down at her. Lucy's expression changed from that of a sweet innocent to hot, aroused woman. His throat closed with some unnamed emotion.

He tossed the packets onto the bed, keeping one for himself, and gazed down at Lucy. Her entire concentration centered completely on his cock, which had the same effect as a lick from her tongue. He held back the need to pounce on top of her, finesse be damned.

"Stand up for me, Lucy," he softly ordered.

To his male delight, she didn't even question his motives. With a subtle kind of grace and fluidity that only Lucy seemed to possess, she did as she was told. Once she was in front of him, he placed the packet in her hands. "Put it on me, sweetheart."

She fiddled with it at first, her nervousness plain. He waited until she had the foil ripped open and had to clench his fists at his sides as she lowered herself to a kneeling position in front of him. She grasped his cock in her warm, delicate hand, looked up at him with a siren's smile curving her plump lips, and licked his dripping tip.

"Goddamn." He wrapped a fist in her hair and guided her over his aching shaft. "Suck it for me good, baby."

She wrapped her arms around his hips and dug her fingers into his buttocks as she swirled her tongue over and around the bulbous head of his penis. Rand lost all semblance of control when she opened wide and slid his engorged cock between her pretty lips. Her moans vibrated along the length of his shaft and nearly had him coming then and there.

She used one talented hand on his balls, fondling and caressing, squeezing just hard enough to draw another groan from deep inside his chest. As he watched her cheeks hollow, sucking hard, he grappled for control. He was too close. Already he could feel his balls drawing up tight. The desire to fill her mouth with his come nearly overrode everything else.

He tugged on her hair and she released him with an audible pop, then leaned back and looked up at him, a secret smile lighting her face. Rand's entire body shook with pleasure as her fingers slowly rolled the condom down his pulsating shaft. It took her a few tries to get it all the way on, which only enhanced the fact that he needed to go slow with her. When she came to her feet, Rand prayed for the power to hold himself in check this first time.

"Was that okay?" she said.

"Are you serious?" He was ready to self-combust!

She looked away and closed her arms over her chest. "It's been—"

He placed two fingers against her lips. "Don't bring the past in here." He didn't want to think about her doing that to any other man. Not fucking ever. "This is about you and me, no one else."

She nodded.

"And I loved it. You just about had me losing it, baby."

"Really?"

"Hell yeah." Jesus, he was so far gone he could barely remember his own name.

He took her arms and nudged her a little, indicating he wanted her to turn around. "Bend over for me, hands on the bed."

She bent forward until her pert round bottom was thrust toward him like a juicy fruit. And he was hungry. Rand stroked his palm over her ass cheeks, then leaned down and bit the creamy flesh.

"Rand!"

He chuckled. "I couldn't resist. You look so tasty."

He wedged a leg between her thighs and forced her open wider. Her thighs trembled, and it cooled him down just enough to slip his finger inside her to test her readiness. He needn't have worried. She was so damn wet and slick there was no possible way he'd hurt her.

Clutching her hips in one hand, he guided his cock to her entrance. Careful not to hurt her, he eased inside her tight passage a few inches, and then stopped, allowing her body to become accustomed to the invasion. She whimpered and he smoothed his palm up her spine, relishing in her silken ivory skin. "Easy. We have all night."

"Oh, God, you feel so good. It's never been this way."

His chest swelled at the confession. "You fit me like a glove. I could stay like this forever."

She threw her head back and Rand watched as she reached a hand between her thighs and grasped his balls in one hand, squeezing. It was the sort of pleasure-pain that sent a man over the edge of control.

"Baby," he groaned.

"Fuck me, Rand. Please don't tease me anymore."

The breathless plea behind her words did him in. He thrust into her in one hard stroke, filling her completely. She cried out his name as he began to move in a rhythm that had her meeting him thrust for thrust. He lowered his body and covered her smaller frame with his own, cuddling and holding her to him as he pushed in and out. Hard and fast, then slow and gentle, playing and tormenting them both with the maddening tempo.

He touched her neck with his tongue and found a particularly sensitive spot that caused Lucy to lay her head to the side and give him access to the pumping vein. He sucked at her tender skin, marking her. Her inner muscles clutched him like a fiery fist as her body spun out of control.

He wrapped his hand loosely around her neck in a dominating hold while she came loud and long for him. Only him. No other.

When she quieted and slumped against the bed, he thrust hard and fast several times, fucking her, filling her so completely she roused and moaned along with him.

"Come for me, Rand," she murmured beneath him.

Her quiet demand was all it took. He lifted her hips and pushed into her tight cunt, fusing them together irrevocably. Arching his neck, he moaned her name as her inner muscles clamped around him, milking his cock. He burned alive as he slammed into her, flesh slapping against flesh. She cried his name and he thrust one last time, then emptied himself into her hot core. He slumped over her, exhausted and sweating.

Rand stayed still for several seconds, wrapped around Lucy, her pussy clutching him in a tender embrace. There was a moment of regret that he'd had to use a condom. He'd never gone without, but with Lucy, there was an overwhelming desire in him to feel her, skin to skin, with nothing separating them.

As he pulled out and stared down at her, his heart swelled. The beautiful, shy, intelligent girl from Ohio was sprawled across his bed, replete, a smile curving her luscious lips. If he had his way she wouldn't be leaving his bed anytime soon.

Fifty years from now, maybe.

Reckless Exposure: Chapter 2

Four Years Later

"Get that camera out of my face or I'll break it."

"Ah, don't be like that, babe."

Lucy stretched her arms over her head as another series of shots were taken. Rand just didn't get the concept of privacy. She tamped down on the extremely feminine reaction she had to the sight of him standing beside the bed totally nude, save for the camera in front of his face. "I've told you before about this, damn it. No pictures before my coffee."

"Slip the sheet down a little, sweetheart."

Lucy knew that tone. He wouldn't budge until he had all the shots he wanted. She sighed and gave into the inevitable. As she pushed the sheet down, baring her nude chest and belly, she heard Rand groan and snap another series of shots. Did the man never tire? They'd had sex three times the night before and still he was ready to party.

"I need to get moving," she warned him. "I've got a shoot today, remember?"

"They can wait. You're so goddamn in demand these

days that I never get to have you all to myself anymore."

He sounded like a wounded animal in need of loving. Lucy couldn't help the zing of pleasure over his possessiveness. "You got me all to yourself last night."

Rand grinned and lowered the camera. "Yeah, I did. And you thought you'd never enjoy anal sex. Guess I proved you wrong there, huh?"

Lucy covered her face. "Must you spell it out?"

She felt the bed dip to one side and soon a hand smoothed over her breast. She peeked between her fingers. Rand's total concentration was centered on her breasts. As he teased his calloused fingers over her nipples, she came alive. He alone had that sort of power over her body. She knew instinctively that no other man would ever make her burn the way he did.

She forced herself to take control of the situation before it got out of hand, which seemed to happen a lot around Rand. She grabbed his hand as he began to massage his way down her belly. "I need to go to work, and unless I'm mistaken, you have a shoot today, too. We need to get our butts in gear."

Rand groaned and pushed his fingers through his hair. "I do need to get ready. Trey bought some monstrous bed and he needs help moving it in. I'm it."

Lucy thought of their mysterious new neighbor. He had a dangerous, rugged appearance with his midnight-black hair and hard, powerful body. He was both hot and scary at the same time. She'd fantasized a few times about Trey. Trey and Rand both. The combination of the two hunks would send a girl's libido right over the moon. "He's so quiet. I'm surprised he asked you for help."

Rand caressed her breast, eliciting a tiny moan from her. "He's a closed-up son-of-a-bitch, that's for sure. I think we're the only ones in the building he's warmed up to."

She had to force herself to stay on the conversation as Rand's fingers flicked over one nipple. "He ever tell you where he came from?" Was that her husky voice?

Rand shook his head and drifted his finger lower, teasing and warming her from the inside out. "Nope, and I don't think he plans to. Something about him says *temporary* to me."

"Yeah, I get that feeling too. And he seems sad, don't you think? As if he's been dealt a raw deal."

Rand nipped her earlobe. "I don't usually ponder another man's feelings, baby."

She laughed and smacked his hand away. "Scoot. I need to get a shower."

He flopped onto the bed and let out a disgusted sigh. "Fine, but tonight you'd better be ready for me."

Her anger rose as she sat up. "I'd better be ready for you? What kind of attitude is that?"

"The attitude of a man who's about a step away from handcuffing his pretty girlfriend to the bed if she doesn't get her ass in the shower."

She shot out of bed. Arrogant man! "Maybe you should be handcuffed to the bed. Then I'd actually get to my shoots on time."

A hand clasped around her middle and pulled her to a stop. Soon she was feeling a pair of lips against the side of her neck. Lucy nearly surrendered. Nearly. She brought her elbow backward and connected with Rand's ribs just hard enough to make a point. He swore and released her.

She whirled on him. "That's for being so arrogant!"

He advanced on her, and the grin on his face wasn't at all reassuring. She took one step back and was turning to sprint into the bathroom when a pair of hands caught her and slung her over a hard, muscled shoulder.

"Put me down right now!" she screamed as she pummeled his back. "You are the most annoying, selfish, barbaric, horny man I know, Rand Miller!"

He set her on her feet inside the bathroom and cupped her chin in his palm. "You are the most gorgeous, intelligent, feisty woman I know, Lucy Flemming."

She narrowed her eyes. What was he up to now? "Flattery won't help you out of this one."

"It's not flattery. It's the truth," he murmured, leaning close to her ear. "And, baby?"

"Yes?" Her voice nearly inaudible as his nearness

began to override her anger.

"I'd better be the *only* horny man you know." He nipped her earlobe, then licked the little sting away.

Before she could gather her wits and retaliate, he was gone, the bathroom door closed. He'd done it again, taken away her ire and replaced it with need. For four years, he'd shown her more pleasure than she ever thought possible. And each time they came together was better than the last. She knew the reason. Love. She loved him with all her heart. Rand wasn't the type a woman fell for, though. She'd known that at the start. He was a daredevil and loved living on the edge, new adventures, new thrills. He would never change, and she had no right to ask him to. She had been the one who'd changed.

She moved to the shower and pushed the curtain aside. As she adjusted the water temperature, she thought about the previous night. They'd both had a long day. She had to fit a shoot between her classes and it had been crazy trying to get from one end of the city to the other. She'd managed it, but barely.

The instant she walked through the apartment door, Rand had been there with a bottle of wine and a bottle of massage oil. He'd worked every last kink out of her tense shoulders and upper back before moving lower. He'd shown her the wicked pleasure of anal sex and her body still vibrated from the intensity of their lovemaking. As she stepped into the shower and let the hot jets of water soothe the delicious aches, she grinned. Lordy, the man was pure sin. Already she wanted him again.

Four years ago last month, she'd come to New York to go to college and be a fashion designer. Four years later, she'd become a successful cover model and was on her way to interning with George Correlli, one of the best designers in the business. She'd already talked to George and he'd agreed to let her do her internship at his company, something he rarely did.

Still, there was something missing. She wanted more. She wanted a home and a family. Kids and a husband who shared in the same simple pleasures of life. Lucy longed for little league games, family dinners, and Friday nights spent watching movies.

Rand would never be content with that kind of life. Two-point-five kids and backyard barbeques were foreign concepts to the boy from Brooklyn whose mother had been a crack-head and whose father had skipped out shortly after he'd turned ten. She knew, because he'd told her that he feared he had the same lousy fathering gene. In a rare moment of weakness, he'd explained how he never wanted to be like his old man, a broke loser who couldn't stand up and be a man for the wife and kid who'd needed him so badly.

She had tried to talk to him about moving their relationship to a more permanent status, but each time she brought up the subject of marriage, he'd start kissing her. Shortly after, they'd be making love, and talks of the future would be put on hold. She was tired of him getting around her with sex. Her mother had gotten married at twenty-five and given birth to her daughter a year later. At twenty-six, Lucy felt her biological clock ticking away.

Even their apartment was a testament to the type of modern, fast lane lifestyle Rand enjoyed. The expensive Italian black leather couch and matching loveseat, coupled with the black glass tiered coffee table screamed "no kids allowed." Their bedroom was no less modern. The king-sized bed with the white leather headboard and red comforter wasn't exactly Homes and Gardens. She loved the furniture they'd chosen for Rand's apartment after she'd moved in, but now that she was thinking about having kids someday, all she saw in her mind was a toddler banging into the sharp corners. Their apartment was a baby's worst nightmare!

Where did that leave her? Did she give up her dreams to keep what they already had? Or was it time to move on? The very idea of never seeing Rand again sat like a lead ball in the pit of her stomach. But what choice did she have?

As she finished, she turned off the shower and stepped out. Lucy nearly fell when she saw Rand sitting on the counter wearing nothing but a pair of black gym shorts and a grin. He was so hard, the all over kind of hard. Six pack abs, large biceps and powerful thighs. The tattoo on his right shoulder did crazy things to her, too. It was an intricate web of black lines and curves. It covered his entire shoulder and snaked down his bicep. He'd told her he'd gotten it right after his first big shoot as a way to celebrate.

Her clit swelled and throbbed as she dripped onto the rug beneath her feet. Rand handed her a towel and pointed to a cup of steaming coffee beside him. She took the towel and wrapped it around her, holding it tight.

"The shower's all yours," she said, still a little perturbed at his high-handedness earlier.

He jumped off the counter and came toward her. When his head descended on hers, the kiss wasn't anything like she expected. It was gentle and sweet, a light mating of lips, no pressure, no demands. She melted.

He lifted away and said, "I'm sorry. Forgive me?"

Yeah, as if any sane woman could stay pissed after that! She pointed a finger at him. "You are dangerous to my health."

He chuckled and smacked her ass as she moved around him. "You're damn lucky Trey's waiting on me."

She turned and glared at him, but he was already naked and slipping into the shower. He heart squeezed tight as the water started up. She couldn't see him through the dark blue curtain, but she could imagine his powerful body, the water sluicing down his chest to his cock. Wet and slippery and edible. Oh God, leaving him would tear her apart. But staying hurt too.

Sometimes life sucked.

***

Lucy loved her classes. She didn't understand why people complained about college. Even as a kid she'd enjoyed learning, a trait that set her apart from most of her classmates. As a result she'd been inducted into the nerdy group. They understood her and appreciated her quirky ways. She slung her purse and satchel over her shoulder and looked at her watch. Four o'clock. Her last class had just let out. As she waited for a cab, someone behind her called her name. She turned to see Trey sprinting toward her.

"Hey, Lucy."

"Hi, Trey. I hear you bought some new furniture," she said, noting his long-sleeved black shirt and snug jeans. He was a powerful man. He had a different build than Rand, but equally powerful. Both men were lean and strong, but Rand's was a street-tough appearance while Trey's aggressive nature concealed itself behind an infectious smile and quiet disposition.

"Yep. I don't know what I would've done if Rand hadn't been there."

"He was glad to do it."

Trey pointed at the large brick building behind her. "Did class just let out?"

"Yeah. If I ever catch a cab, I might actually make it home before midnight," she grumbled as yet another cab sped by, ignoring her completely. "I should just take the subway."

Trey placed his hand on her elbow. "You have a few minutes for a cup of coffee?"

She searched his face for signs he was hitting on her. When all she saw was a friend offering to buy her cup of coffee, she smiled. "Sure. I could use the caffeine fix."

They started down the street in silence. As they came upon a little coffee shop that boasted the best beans in New York, Trey stopped and held the door for her.

"Thanks," she said, appreciating the fact that some men still held doors for women. She wasn't seeing nearly enough of that sort of thing since leaving her small town in Ohio.

Spotting an empty table, she headed toward it. Their waitress took their order and quickly went off to fill it, leaving Lucy with a silent and watchful Trey.

"Rand and I were talking about you the other day," she blurted out, needing to break the uncomfortable moment.

"Is that right?" Trey said as their coffee arrived. He thanked their waitress, who promptly began to stutter and tremble, clearly taken with him.

Lucy poured cream in hers and noticed as Trey dumped four packets of sugar in his. The man must have a terrific metabolism. "Yeah, we were just saying that you're awfully quiet. You don't socialize much. Have you made many friends since you moved here?"

"Nah, I try to keep a low profile. You and Rand are enough for me."

"Wouldn't a single guy like you rather hang out where he might see some action?"

He chuckled. "Action? You have no idea how much action I've seen over the years, Lucy. Action isn't all it's cracked up to be."

She couldn't seem to stop herself from asking, "Do you have a girlfriend tucked away?"

Trey stayed quiet as he stirred his coffee. Finally he said, "No, there's no one for me. Sometimes it's best that way."

"Maybe you just aren't looking in the right place," she said softly, hating the note of sadness in his voice. It seemed wrong for a guy like Trey to be alone. Surely women drooled over him everywhere he went, so why was he single?

"I've got too much unfinished business, Lucy. Until it's settled, there won't be any Mrs. Trey Madison to warm my sheets." He paused before adding, "Besides, I stay pretty busy counseling."

"Counseling?"

"Yeah, I counsel couples."

She perked up at the prospect of learning more about him. "Like a marriage counselor?"

He grinned. "More of a sex therapist."

Lucy blushed. "Oh."

Trey winked at her. "You and Rand won't be needing counseling, that's for sure. Now there's a marriage waiting to happen."

She cringed and looked away. "No. Rand doesn't do marriage."

He cupped her chin and forced her to look at him, his eyes full of tenderness. "You're so sure?"

She nodded. "Yeah. Rand likes to live on the edge. He's too wild to ever consider marriage."

"Don't sell him short, Lucy. He may surprise you."

She didn't want to let herself hope. As the waitress came to deliver their bill, she let out a sigh of relief. Trey grabbed it before she could reach for the scrap of paper.

He stood. "I can buy you a cup of coffee, Lucy."

She thanked him before he turned and strode toward the register to pay. She couldn't help but watch him walk. He was so well built! Was it such a crime to look? She finished the last of her coffee and scooted her own chair back. Grabbing her purse and satchel, she followed Trey out of the little shop. He walked her to the curb and hailed a cab for her. As it pulled alongside, she smiled up at him.

"If you're going back to the apartment, we could share?"

Trey held the door for her and shook his head.

"Nope. I have a few more errands to run before I head home."

"Well, thanks for the coffee then. And the conversation."

"Ditto," he said before adding, "and Lucy?"

"Yes?"

"Think about what I said. There's nothing in the world worse than looking back and knowing you made the wrong decision."

She didn't have to wonder what he meant. He was talking about Rand. Trey was convinced Rand would marry her. Why he felt so strongly about it was a mystery. Trey didn't know him the way she did. Still, a small kernel of hope seemed to take up residence in her heart.

As she waved Trey off, her cell phone rang. The special ring tone meant it was Rand. "Hello?"

"Hey, babe, you busy?"

His deep, hoarse voice always sent butterflies flitting through her stomach. "I just finished. I'm heading home. Want me to stop and get anything on the way?"

"Don't bother. I was thinking of taking you to that Chinese restaurant you love so much. Are you in the mood for chow mein?"

"Definitely, and I don't have another shoot for several weeks, so I can even pig out."

Someone tapped on the cab window, startling her. "Hang on a sec," she said into the phone. Lucy turned her head to see Luke Riley, one of her classmates, grinning in at her. She rolled the window down.

"Hey, Lucy," he said in a breathless voice as he hunkered down so they were eye to eye. "Me and some of the others are getting together at Connolly's. Want to come?"

Connolly's was their favorite pub hangout. She'd been there a few times, but usually she was too anxious to get home to Rand. "Thanks, Luke, but I've already got plans." She smiled to take the sting out of her rejection. "You'll just have to have fun without me."

He grinned as he slung his computer bag over his shoulder and began walking backward down the street. "One of these days I'm going to show you what you've been missing," he called out to her.

Lucy laughed, waved him off, and rolled the window back up. The cabby cleared his throat as if getting annoyed, so she rattled off her address and went back to her conversation with Rand. "Sorry. That was someone from my art class."

"I heard. He was asking you out."

He sounded jealous. She'd rarely heard Rand jealous. He would get a little possessive at times, but jealousy was never a big issue between them. "Not really. He was asking me to go out with him and the rest of the group."

"The group thing is an excuse, Lucy. Trust me. He wants you."

She thought of Luke. He did tend to flirt with her quite a bit. At first she thought it was because she was a model. Some men thought scoring with a model gave them extra points or something. It was annoying as hell. But Luke had asked her out on more than one occasion. Even though she always declined, he persisted and seemed genuinely interested in her. "Maybe, but it doesn't matter, because I turned him down."

"I still want to hit him. Doesn't he know you're taken?"

"Of course he knows. Everyone at school knows about you. I'm always bragging about the hot photographer I live with."

Rand chuckled. "This hot photographer is hungry, and I'm not talking about the chow mein either."

Her temperature spiked. "Be good."

"I'm always good."

His voice skated over her body in an erotic caress. "I think you're very, very bad," she whispered, hoping the cabbie couldn't hear.

"Come home, baby. I miss you."

She forced herself to remember her determination to talk to Rand. She needed to put her life on track. She couldn't live the carefree cover-model existence forever. She needed stability. Love. A family. It was now or never. She wanted what her parents had, kids and a loving relationship that could withstand the test of time. And if she couldn't have that, then it was time to move on.

"Rand, we need to talk. Tonight."

There was silence over the line for several seconds and Lucy was afraid the call had been lost. "That sounds serious," he finally said, his voice filled with concern.

Oh god, her heart hurt. It actually hurt. She'd put that note of concern in his voice. How would she ever be able to move out if just hearing his voice had her second-guessing herself? "I'll talk to you when I get home, okay?"

"You know I care about you, right?"

Care, not love. He'd never once said the 'L' word. "I know, Rand."

"Be careful."

"I will."

They ended the call and Lucy felt the first tear trail down her cheek. This wasn't going to be easy. In fact, it just might kill her.

Reckless Exposure: Chapter 3

She wanted to talk. That couldn't be good. Rand paced the length of the living room as he imagined every scenario known to man and came up empty. He couldn't figure what he'd done wrong, and surely he'd done something. Women didn't say they needed to talk if there wasn't something pissing them off. Lucy rarely got mad at him, though, and more often than not, she talked it out with him.

From the minute she'd come awake to his camera snapping in her face, he'd known something was off. She'd been different. He shouldn't have tried to take her picture before she'd had her coffee. He knew better, damn it. She'd just been so fucking adorable, like a sweet angel from heaven in his bed. He loved watching her sleep. She snored a little and hogged the blankets, but he wouldn't have it any other way. With Lucy cuddled up to his side, Rand slept like the dead. He was a hard man, used to life delivering him the shitty end of the stick, but with Lucy he felt happy, warm and content. He'd die without her.

He shoved his fingers through his hair and paced some more. When he heard the key slide into the lock, his heart nearly stopped beating. Lucy strode in and smiled at him, but there wasn't any light behind the action and she looked as if she'd been crying. Damn, what the hell had he done?

He went to her and took her in his arms. Her body melted against him for a few seconds before she pulled away. She put her keys on the table next to the door and set her purse and satchel on the floor. Rand waited, unsure what to do or say. As she perched on the edge of the couch, he walked silently to the chair facing her and sat on the arm.

"I don't know how to say this, except to just say it." She wrung her fingers together and kept her head down.

Both gestures were very bad signs. "You can tell me anything," he encouraged. "Talk to me, Lucy."

"I want to know where I stand with you. We've been together four years, Rand. Four wonderful years, but where is this relationship headed?"

He knelt on the floor in front of her and took her hand in his. Entwining their fingers together seemed as natural as breathing. "You're my girl, Lucy. I care about you. I don't see what the problem is here. Things are great the way they are. Why fix it if it's not broken, angel?"

Her eyes pleading with him, she tucked a stray hair behind her ear. "I want to be more than your girlfriend. Don't you think it's time to talk about the future? Our future?"

"Are you so sure you want to change this, baby?" The Miller men weren't cut out to be husbands. Rand leaned down and placed a gentle kiss to the back of her hand. He kept his gaze locked on hers as he trailed kisses from the inside of her wrist to her elbow. Lucy shuddered and tried to pull her hand away, but he was quicker, stronger. He held her firm and cupped the back of her head with his palm. "Why chance ruining a good thing?"

He pulled her forward and pressed his lips to hers, relishing the way her breath hitched. Her mouth opened, inviting him in. He took the advantage and allowed his tongue to duel with hers. He coasted his palm down her back before slipping around the front to cup one firm breast through her blouse. Without warning she jerked backwards, her eyes narrowing.

"Damn it, Rand, you do this every single time!"

He stood, his own anger pushing to the surface. "What the hell are you talking about? Do what?"

"Try to wiggle out of talking about marriage. Don't deny it. You always get around me with sex. Well, not this time. I won't let you seduce me into forgetting about our future."

"We have a good thing. What the hell is wrong with letting things go on as they are?"

She shook her head and looked down at the floor, her body slumping as if in defeat. "I think I need to move out."

His entire body went rigid. He couldn't have heard her right. "What did you say?"

She finally lifted her head, her soft eyes full of tears. "I think it's time we call it quits."

His life was suddenly spiraling out of control, and he had no idea why. His temper flared. "What the fuck for?"

Lucy flinched and stayed silent.

He went to her, unable to stand the distance another second. He crouched in front of her and placed his hand on her knee. "I'm sorry. I didn't mean to shout at you. But you can't mean that. You're angry."

"Rand, please understand. You really are wonderful, but I need more than a boyfriend. I want a husband."

"Can you honestly tell me you're ready to walk away from what we have, Lucy?"

"I-I want to get married. I want to have babies some day. I need to be more than a cover model. I'm twenty-six years old. It's time I started thinking about the future."

He got to his feet and stepped backwards. Marriage and babies. There it was, the warped image of his own childhood. As if it were yesterday, he could see his mother's crazed eyes as she shouted at his father. Every time she came down off a high, Rand's life would turn to shit. She'd lash out at anything and anyone as she suffered through the withdrawal. He'd often gotten in the way of her flying fists when he was too small to defend himself. Later, as his body matured, she'd use words to hurt him, knowing she was no longer strong enough to confront him physically. What the hell did he know about family? He hadn't seen his mother since he turned eighteen and left home. His father had deserted them long before that.

He went to the window and stared down at the street. He saw a few teenagers standing around, chatting and texting on cell phones. A woman pushing a stroller walked by and Rand's gut clenched. Lucy wanted babies. He could already see her pregnant. She'd be a wonderful mother. But she couldn't possibly want him as the father. He was a piece of dirt from the streets of Brooklyn. Maybe she had someone else in mind already. Did she have someone willing to fill in as husband and daddy once he was out of the picture?

"When did you decide all this?" he asked as he continued to watch the woman until she rounded a corner and went out of sight. He didn't trust himself to turn and face Lucy. He wasn't ready to see the knowledge in her eyes that he wasn't good enough to father her children.

"It's not something I came up with on a whim. I've been thinking about it for a while now."

He swiveled and pinned her with a hard glare. "You've been sharing my bed, all the while knowing you would be leaving me soon? You knew last night? We made love, Lucy! Three damn times!"

She stood then, her back stiff with anger. "Like I said, I've tried to talk to you about this several times, but you always change the subject. Don't lie. You know you do. And while we're at it, can you honestly stand there and tell me you love me? That you would want to marry me and have babies with me?"

He took two steps toward her and pointed a finger at her. "You aren't exactly over the hill, Lucy. There's still plenty of time to consider marriage and kids." He paused as a painful thought hit him. "Maybe the real problem here is that you've already decided I wasn't good enough for the long haul. A street punk. Is that all I am to you?"

She blanched. "Of course not. I love you. I always have."

He closed the distance between them and caught her arms before she could turn away. "Have you found someone else? Is it that asshole I heard on the phone?"

Lucy pushed at his chest, but he refused to budge. "It's not like that. There is no one else!"

"So for four years I was a good enough to fuck, but now it's time to move on."

He knew the instant he'd pushed too far. She clenched her fists at her sides and angry sparks flew from her gorgeous brown eyes.

"Do not put words in my mouth. You're the one dodging discussions of the future, not me. You're the one who can't get over the past, not me. You're the one who can't admit you love me, not me. You're the one who swore never to have kids for fear you'd be just like your father. Not me!"

He released her and stumbled backwards. Every single word she'd thrown at him was right on the mark. She was leaving him, and he'd pushed her to it. He had no one to blame but himself. He'd kept her at arm's length for four years. No self-respecting woman could put up with that type of treatment forever.

"Rand?"

Her pleading voice was too much. He shook his head and headed for the door. He needed time to think, to figure out how to fix the mess he'd made. To figure out how to keep the woman he loved from walking away and leaving him a shell of a man.

"Rand, please talk to me," she said as he slung the door wide.

"I need a few minutes, Lucy." If she said anything else, he didn't hear it. All he heard was his own inner voice lecturing him on his idiocy. Rand closed the door behind him and started down the hall. He wasn't watching where he was going and smacked head-on into someone.

"Hey, Trey. Sorry about that. I wasn't paying attention," he mumbled.

Trey quirked a brow. "I gathered. Something wrong?"

Wrong? His entire life was going down the goddamn

toilet! "Yeah, you could say that."

"Come on." Trey smacked him on the back. "I've got a few beers in the fridge."

Rand wasn't the sharing type, but Trey had already moved around him and started down the hall. He shrugged. What the hell? Maybe if he got drunk enough he wouldn't have to think about Lucy marrying some dickwad and living in the fucking 'burbs.

Rand walked into Trey's living room and shook his head at the peculiar furnishings. He had a hodgepodge of stuff and nothing seemed to match, yet it all looked damned expensive. Antiques from around the world filled the room. An old roll top desk from the early 1900s. A rosewood bookcase that had such intricate carvings Rand thought it had come straight from China. A pair of mahogany end tables and an oak-and-glass corner cabinet that was filled with nothing but crystal. He'd bet his last dollar it wasn't the cheap shit either. He'd known for a while that Trey counseled couples in trouble, but now he wondered if Trey was also a collector, though he didn't really strike Rand as the type of guy to go antiquing. Damn, helping couples work out their problems must be a lucrative business.

In the kitchen, Trey tossed him a beer and grabbed one for himself.

Rand popped the top and drank half the bottle before setting it on the counter.

"So, what's eating you?"

That was Trey, straight to the point. "Lucy wants to move out." Even saying the words hurt. He couldn't imagine a future without her. His blood ran cold just thinking of her waking up to someone else every morning. Sharing a pot of coffee and fighting over the last donut with some man who could give her what she wanted. A future.

Trey leaned against the counter. "She say why?"

"She seems to think I'm not the marrying kind." Rand pushed his fingers through his hair as his mind played back the argument with Lucy. "We've been together four years. I never figured on her ending it like this."

"She wants a ring on her finger, but not your ring?"

"Not exactly. She's tried to talk to me about marriage before. I've gotten good at getting her to change the subject."

"So you're the one with cold feet, huh?"

"Lucy wants a man who can be a father to the kids she dreams of having," Rand said. "I'm not cut out for that job."

"Why not? You don't want kids?"

He knew Trey was just trying to help, but talking about his past wasn't something Rand was ever comfortable with. He hadn't even told Lucy everything. He'd skated over the details because he hadn't wanted to dredge up bad memories. Looking down at the floor, he shoved his hands in the pockets of his jeans. "It's in my DNA. The Miller men suck at being husbands and fathers. My dad skipped out when I was ten. His dad beat the shit out of him every chance he got. I come from a long line of deadbeat dads. It's best if I end the cycle here."

The silence that followed his speech lasted so long that Rand lifted his head to see if Trey had left the room. He hadn't.

"We have to walk our own path," Trey said, his face devoid of emotion. "*You* decide the kind of father you'll be. No one else."

Rand didn't agree. "I don't trust myself with kids."

"You're using the past as an excuse not to deal with your problems. It'll only make things worse."

Trey's words pricked Rand's temper. "What the hell do you know about it?"

"What, you think I just fell out of the sky?" Trey pointed at his own chest. "I know a thing or two about relationships. Besides, I have my own fair share of skeletons. But if I let other people's mistakes dictate my future, who's the fool then?"

He knew Trey counseled couples in trouble, but Rand's demons went deeper than most. "Hell, I don't know. All I do know is that I can't lose her. I'd be lost without her."

"Do you love her?"

"Yeah, I do, and it scares the shit out of me."

"Have you told her that?"

"She should know how I feel. I show her every day!"

Trey crossed his arms over his chest. "Women like to hear the words."

But that was part of the problem. Rand couldn't say the words. He'd never been able to say them. The one time his father had said those words, he'd left the next day and he never come back. "I'm not sure it would matter. She's dead set on moving out. She wants things I'm not sure I can give her."

"Then maybe the best thing to do is let her go."

Hearing Trey say what he had already been thinking made Rand sick to his stomach. Lucy deserved better. It was selfish of him to hold onto her. "Damn, this sucks."

"Give her a going away present."

Was the man insane? "A present? She's leaving me and you want me to buy her a fucking gift?"

"Not a gift from a store, bonehead. Something more personal than that. Fulfill her wildest fantasy or something."

Rand shook his head. "Jesus, you really are nuts."

Trey grinned and took a swig of his beer. "Maybe. But if you care about Lucy, don't let her leave with a heart filled with regrets and what-ifs. Give her a night to remember. Come on, what's her wildest fantasy?"

Rand didn't have to think on it. He already knew. She'd revealed it to him once after a few margaritas. His heart swelled as he thought of that night. It didn't take much to get Lucy tipsy. She was a total lightweight. Plus, she got really horny, a definite plus.

"She was buzzed once and told me she's always dreamed of being with two men at once," Rand admitted.

Trey's gaze lit up. "Think you can give her that?"

"Why would I even want to?" Rand imagined Lucy sandwiched between himself and some faceless stranger. He'd never thought the scenario would appeal to him, but knowing how much pleasure Lucy would derive from the act held a hell of a lot of appeal. Still, could he stand to let another man's cock anywhere near Lucy's soft supple body? Hell, no.

"So, Lucy's really fantasized about a threesome?"

Rand narrowed his eyes. "You sound intrigued."

Trey's expression lightened. "Of course I'm intrigued. Lucy is a beautiful woman. Besides, I am a sex therapist."

Realization dawned. "The hands-on kind?"

Trey's gaze never wavered from his. "My sessions are private."

Rand didn't pry. He wasn't sure he wanted to know. "And you think I'd let you be our third?"

Trey tsked. "That's not up to either of us, now, is it? It's up to Lucy. It's what she wants that matters here."

"Bullshit. You want to fuck my girlfriend." Rand's anger rose as an image sprang to mind of a naked Lucy touching and kissing Trey.

"Half the United States wants to fuck your girlfriend, Rand," Trey shot right back. "She's sexy as sin. Besides being gorgeous, she's also smart and a genuinely nice person. Do you really think I've not thought about it? Shit, I'm not dead!"

Rand slammed his beer bottle on the counter and moved toward Trey. He grabbed the other man by his shirtfront and yanked him close. "Keep away from Lucy."

Trey held up his hands as if in surrender. "I'm not angling to take your place here. Ease the hell up."

Rand released him and stepped back. "I'm beginning to think the only reason you even brought up the idea of fulfilling Lucy's fantasies was so you could get some pussy. But let me set you straight on that score. Lucy is mine, and I don't fucking share."

Trey rolled his eyes. "You stupid son of a bitch. What will you do when she leaves you, huh? Beat the shit out of every guy she takes an interest in?"

Rand hadn't let himself think that far. He was still trying to figure out how he was going to live without her. "If I have to, yeah."

"Give me a break. You can't hold onto her by bulldozing. You're going to have to suppress that hard-ass nature of yours and give Lucy something special, something that proves you can be the man she craves."

"And giving her a night with you is just the ticket? That's the craziest thing I've ever heard."

"Not me. *Us.*"

Rand still hesitated, though he wanted to strangle the man in front of him. Then again, it didn't hurt to let him have his say before Rand buried him six feet under.

"Think about what Lucy wants for a minute, not what your possessive streak wants."

Rand crossed his arms over his chest. "Let me ask you this, all knowing one. If you had a woman, would you be so keen on the idea of another man having sex with her?"

Trey hesitated, as if warring with himself. "No, I wouldn't be. It's not that I don't feel you, man, I do. But sometimes you have to fight a hard battle in order to reap the rewards."

"That's real philosophical of you, pal. But I still want to punch you."

"Fine. Then think of it this way. You give Lucy this one night of pleasure, which is something she's always imagined, and it opens the door to more fantasies being fulfilled."

"What do you mean?"

"Can you tell me you've never fantasized about doing certain things with Lucy?"

"Sure, but I know she would never go for it."

Trey arched a brow. "She might, especially after you prove to her that you can lock your alpha beast in the cage for a night. She'll be forced to trust you in the same way you're trusting her."

Trey had a valid point. But if he chose to take Trey up on his offer, he took the chance of losing Lucy to the other man. On top of that, it would also permanently change their relationship. There would be no going back for either of them. Did he dare risk it?

"What do you really have to lose?" Trey asked, as if reading his mind. "She's already said she's leaving. Give her a reason to stay. Give her your complete trust."

Rand knew Trey was right and it sucked. "She does think you're hot," he blurted out.

Trey laughed. "Glad to hear it."

Rand shouldn't smile, but for some reason he was beginning to feel less threatened by Trey. He'd seen men try to get in Lucy's pants, hundreds of times. It always set his teeth on edge. But Trey made it clear he wasn't looking to take his place.

"If I do this, I wouldn't want there to be any misunderstandings," Rand warned. "It would be for one night only. No coming back for more later."

"Of course."

"And you leave right after. I don't want Lucy embarrassed."

"Give me some credit here. I'm not a complete ass. I would never hurt Lucy."

Rand stepped up to the counter and took the last few swigs of his beer before saying, "Come over tomorrow night. I'll let Lucy know you're there to hang out. We'll see how things go. We let Lucy choose how the night ends."

Trey nodded. "What time?"

"Be there at seven."

"Okay."

Neither of them said another word. Rand let himself out. As he headed to his own apartment, one question kept running through his mind.

What the hell have I just agreed to?

Reckless Exposure: Chapter 4

Lucy had spent nearly ten minutes staring at the door after Rand left. The stricken look on his face would forever be etched into her mind. She hadn't meant to hurt him. She loved him, more than she ever thought she could love anyone. Why couldn't he love her back? The phone rang, pulling her from her morose thoughts. She went to the end table and picked up the cordless.

"Hello?"

"Hi, sweetie."

Her throat clogged with emotion. Her legs gave out and she dropped onto the couch. "Mom."

"What's wrong? And don't say nothing. I can hear it in your tone."

It was always that way with her mother. She knew when something wasn't right. "Rand and I had a fight."

"You told him you wanted to move out?"

She'd already poured out her worries to her mother. She'd surprised Lucy when she'd sworn Rand would do the right thing and marry her. "Yeah."

"Honey, this may be hard to hear, but I think you're misjudging him. I don't think he's quite the wild daredevil you think. Are you certain he doesn't love you?"

Lucy hated having to say it aloud. It just seemed to hurt worse. "He cares about me, probably more than he's ever cared about a woman. But I don't think he loves me."

"I'm so sorry, honey. Maybe you need a break. You should come home for a few days. It might help to clear your head."

"I can't right now. I can maybe get away in a few weeks, when Thanksgiving break comes up." She sniffled. "But I need to deal with this on my own. I can't run home every time something doesn't go my way."

"I understand, but I'm here if you want to talk or cry. Okay?"

"Thanks, Mom." She heard the doorknob rattle. "I need to go. He's back."

"All right then. Have patience, Lucy. It'll all work out. You'll see."

"I love you," Lucy said.

"I love you too."

They ended the call just as Rand came through the door. He looked tired and worried. Guilt swamped her. She stood and went to him.

"You were never a street punk to me," Lucy said as she wrapped her arms around her middle in an effort to keep from reaching for him.

Rand stared down at her, his gaze unreadable,

before he took her into his arms and held her tight. His warmth surrounded her and made her feel whole and safe. She always felt protected in Rand's arms, as if nothing bad could ever touch her.

"Don't move out too soon," he said. "Give me time to think. Just a little time. Okay, babe?"

Lucy nodded and buried her face against his shirt.

"I've got some things I need to work out on my own," he admitted. "Please understand."

She pushed back a few inches and looked up at him. "I never planned to leave right away. I don't even have a plan."

He cupped her chin in his palm. "Come to bed with me. I need to hold you, baby."

"Yes," she said on a sigh.

Before she knew what he was about, he had her in his arms, cradled against the hard, muscled plains of his chest. He went straight to their bedroom and placed her in the center of the bed. He stood back and started undressing. Lucy couldn't move. He pulled his t-shirt from the waistband of his jeans, yanked it over his head and flung it to the floor. She wanted to lick him. He was so delicious. As he started on his jeans, Lucy's breath caught. She couldn't pull her gaze away as the material parted, revealing a pair of black boxer briefs beneath. Fascinated by the package he unwrapped, Lucy forgot about their argument, the worries about her future. Everything fell away in the face of her mounting desire.

"Get undressed for me, angel."

She licked her lips and nearly missed his command as he slid his jeans and boxer briefs down his powerful thighs. The sight of him nude always sent her libido into orbit. There was nothing like seeing Rand wild and turned on. Tonight he seemed especially intense.

She lifted to a sitting position and unbuttoned her red blouse. Rand didn't move, didn't speak. His blue eyes darkened as she pulled the delicate fabric away from her body, revealing a red satin camisole beneath. His fists clenched as she pulled it off.

"You're so fucking beautiful. Every inch of you is pure heaven, baby."

His words sent a zing of pleasure through her. She'd heard others say she was pretty. Her entire life, she'd been praised for her looks. She had never needed the flattery. She wanted people to see beyond the shell to the woman beneath. When Rand paid her compliments, she knew he saw more than a well-toned body. He saw her soul, and that made her *feel* beautiful.

She unzipped and tugged and soon her black slacks and panties lay at the end of the bed. She lay back against the comforter and waited, curious what Rand would do next. She couldn't get a handle on his mood this time. The way his gaze roamed over her body brought goose bumps to the surface. She'd never seen him appear so savage, as if their earlier argument had torn down the civil veneer he always kept in place.

Rand wrapped his fist around his cock and pumped once. "Come here."

Lucy didn't hesitate. She wanted to get closer to Rand. Closer to all that male perfection. She needed to touch him, taste him. She scooted across the cool surface of the bed until she sat at the edge, her legs dangling over the side.

Rand stepped closer and bent at the knees. "Taste my cock, Lucy," he demanded. "Do it now, before I lose my mind and shove it between those pretty lips of yours."

"You would never hurt me, Rand." As the words left her mouth she wasn't sure which one of them she was reassuring.

He cupped her chin and leaned down. "I'm not a good little farm boy from Ohio, Lucy. Like it or not, I am a street punk from Brooklyn. Know this. I will not give you up without a fight, sweetheart, and I fight dirty."

Lucy's entire body flooded with heat at his guttural words. "I don't know what you want from me, Rand," she confessed. All the times they'd made love, he had always been gentle, sweet and giving. Now she witnessed a side to him she never knew existed.

"It's simple. Open your soft lips and take my cock down that pretty throat of yours," he ordered.

She reached up and stroked her fingers over his soft

balls. She bit her lip as she stared up at him. She was way out of her comfort zone, as if someone had suddenly tossed her into the middle of the woods without a compass.

He wrapped his fist in her hair and pulled gently at the silken strands. "You say you love me, Lucy. Show me how much. Put the good little small town girl away for tonight and bring me the hot, willful vixen that stood up to me earlier."

Lucy shook her head as panic started to course through her. "I'm not a vixen. I'm just me. You know that. You've seen the real me. Felt the real me. There isn't anything else to it."

His fingers loosened and he kneaded her scalp with his callused fingers. "There's so much more to you, baby. Stop hiding from me. You want it? Then take it."

Her control snapped. "You are the most infuriating man I have ever known!" She started to move backwards, but he was quicker. He wrapped his hands around her thighs and held her still, keeping her from retreating. "Let me go, damn you."

"Ah, there's my little wildcat. Does it make you mad, Lucy? Wanting me so badly that your pussy is soaking wet, your nipples are tight and hard, but you're too much the coward to take me. Sucks, huh?"

His sideways grin did things to her, made her ache so much she nearly begged, which only served to piss her off further. She tried to kick him, but he evaded her easily. "I'm not a coward. You're just being a bully. You're mad that I want to move out, so you're punishing me."

He released one thigh and caressed her mound. "No, I'm making you see that what we have together can't be had with anyone else. I'm it for you and you're it for me. There is no one else who can make you burn like I can." He slid one finger between her pussy lips and she fairly moaned at the sweet torture. "There will never be another woman to turn me inside out the way you do, Lucy. Walk away from that and you're condemning us both to live a half-life. Can't you see that?"

Lucy could barely maintain the thread of the conversation with Rand's finger sinking deep. As she looked into his eyes, she saw it. Fear. Rand was scared. She could see it in the angry set of his jaw. She'd never seen Rand afraid, not of anything. She'd once thought the man could face down an entire gang on his own and still not break a sweat. Yet the thought of losing her had made him afraid? The knowledge dispelled her anger as nothing else could have done.

She let the tension seep out of her and knew Rand saw the change at once. Neither of them spoke as she reached up and took his heavy erection in her hand and squeezed. "I'm not a coward." She stroked her thumb over the head of his cock.

"Fuck, Lucy."

A second finger joined the first inside her aching

pussy. Lucy threw her head back and moaned at the sensual torture. Rand was there in an instant. He pulled his fingers free and framed her face with his large hands. "Do you want me? Just me?"

"Yes, Rand. Please, I need you so much it hurts."

"Lie back on the bed, baby."

Beyond denying anything he asked, Lucy obeyed. The only thing that mattered was Rand filling her, making her feel warm again.

He pushed her thighs wide and knelt between them. He placed a gentle kiss to her clit before murmuring, "You owe me a sucking. Don't think I've forgotten, angel."

She wanted to speak, really she did, but as his tongue sank into her hot center, she gave up on words and let her senses take over.

A primitive growl reverberated inside Rand's chest at the way Lucy's body moved against his face. When he parted her with his fingers and sank his tongue even deeper into her hot opening, she moaned his name and grasped onto his head as if afraid he'd disappear.

Christ, she was so fucking responsive. He loved that about Lucy. The slightest touch could have her melting against him. He imagined her coming apart tomorrow night in Trey's arms. A powerful mix of tenderness and possessiveness threatened to engulf him. He wanted to please her, make her wildest fantasy come to life, but the need to keep her all to himself was overwhelming.

He slid his tongue in and out of her creamy slit, slowly working her into a frenzy, then used his thumb to stroke over the delicate bud of nerves. He licked and nibbled, torturing her flesh until she started to beg for release. Her cries filled him and took away the fears of losing her. The only thing that mattered was watching Lucy scream out her climax as her hot juices poured over his tongue. It wasn't enough. He was starving for the feel of her cunt as she closed around his engorged cock.

He leaned back on his haunches. "On your hands and knees now."

"I can't move, Rand. It's impossible after that climax."

He chuckled at Lucy's drowsy tone. "Sure it is, angel." She looked so sweet and vulnerable in that moment right after a climax. Her defenses were shredded. His protective instincts kicked in. He slid his fingers over her torso as if memorizing her. Their suddenly very unknown future had him anxious to capture and treasure each moment with her.

He made his way to her breasts, pinching one raspberry nipple between his finger and thumb. Lucy whimpered. He leaned down and licked the other, suckling her silky flesh. She pushed her tits against his face as if aching for more. He cupped both tempting orbs, pushing them together, and nuzzled her cleavage. "So sweet and soft. I love your pretty tits."

"I love you, Rand."

Every muscle in his body pulled tight at those precious words. Each time she said them it tore a path through his soul. He wanted to say them back as much as he wanted to take his next breath. But his past reared its ugly head every time, so he always held back. And he'd called her the coward! He was a spineless ass for letting the woman of his heart even consider walking away, and all because he was so fucked up that he couldn't even tell her how he felt.

Rand forced everything out of his mind save for cherishing Lucy. He wrapped his hands around her middle and turned her to her stomach before forcing her up to her knees. With her ass facing him, his cock flexed as if desperate to sink deep.

"Now, Rand," she moaned. "I need you now."

"The first time I saw you, I wanted to fuck you," he told her. "Did you know that?"

"No," she said. "I didn't know."

He reached for the condom he'd pulled from his pocket earlier and sheathed himself. He stroked her ass cheeks, then swatted her. She yelped. "I watched you walk. Your sexy ass teased the hell out of me. I ached to reach out and squeeze." Positioning his cock against her slick folds, he rubbed up and down, barely grazing her clit. Then he slipped inside a scarce inch before moving back out and doing it all over again.

"Oh, God, Rand! You're driving me crazy. I want you

inside me so badly."

He watched as he moved his cock in a slow, gentle glide that nearly had them both rocketing out of control. "Not just yet, baby."

"Damn you! Fuck me, Rand."

He swatted her ass once more, mesmerized as much by the sounds coming from Lucy as the flesh of her ass turning a pretty shade of pink. "You like that?"

"You've never been like this before. Stop teasing me."

He used his other hand to reach beneath her and fondle her breast. "You've never threatened to leave me before. I guess it's a day for firsts."

Lucy stayed silent as she pushed against his cock, attempting to take her own pleasure. Rand swatted her two more times, then leaned close to her ear and demanded, "Admit you like it, Lucy. You like it when I get rough. Say it."

"You turn me inside out. You make me want things, forbidden things."

He smoothed her hair away from her face and kissed the side of her neck. "Sometimes it feels good to be a little naughty. Sometimes gentle just isn't enough."

Rand lifted back up and plunged deep. Her tight pussy closed around him like a vise, and it was all he could do to keep from coming. She pushed backwards, impaling herself further, and he lost the last thread of his control. Rand thrust into her, hard and fast, fucking her with more force than he'd ever used with any woman. He held her still as he slammed against her hips, burying his cock inside the warm depths of her body. Her lush curves trembled and vibrated just for him. All for him.

"Lucy." Her name and nothing more. It was all he was capable of in that moment. She had him in her fiery grip. Lucy spun out of control, her sweet cream bathing his cock, and Rand let himself go in a driving need to fill her, mark her. Three more thrusts and he was spilling his come deep.

He collapsed over her, exhausted and spent. She wiggled and he forced himself to loosen the hold he had on her body. As he lifted away, she rolled to her back and stared up at him. Her flushed cheeks and sated body had his heart swelling. She was so gorgeous. So perfect for him. How would he find the strength to let her go?

"You're a wild man."

Her husky voice had him grinning. She would have a sore throat after all the screaming she'd done. He knew she referred to the spanking he'd given her. She liked it, though she wasn't quite ready to admit it yet. He placed his hands on the bed either side of her head and leaned down. "It's your fault. With that yummy body and those wicked chocolate-brown eyes, a man is helpless."

When he kissed her, she wrapped her arms around

his head and opened for him. He didn't plunge into her mouth, but rather teased her lips and let her come to him. As her tongue dipped shyly into his mouth, he knew a truth he'd been denying himself. Somehow, some way, he'd have to face the past. If he didn't, he was going to lose everything that mattered.

Rand lifted away and went to the bathroom to dispose of the condom. He came back and sprawled on the bed next to Lucy, dragging the blanket over them both. As he pulled her to his side, he felt himself relax. Just before she slipped into sleep, he said, "Trey's coming over tomorrow night."

Lucy stiffened. "He is?"

Interesting reaction. "Yeah. I thought we could get some stuff from the store, maybe make margaritas. Sound good?"

Several seconds passed before she nodded. "It sounds like fun. I can make fajitas, too, if you want."

Rand's arm tightened around her before he was even aware of it. His possessive instincts were already kicking in, and they hadn't even gotten to the threesome. Fuck! He forced himself to relax. It would all work out. It had to. He could give her this fantasy. He was man enough to put his baggage aside and think only of Lucy.

If he told himself that about a million more times, maybe he'd even believe it.

Reckless Exposure: Chapter 5

After several fajitas, Rand sat back and patted his stomach. "I'm stuffed. That was damned delicious, Lucy."

Trey swiped a napkin across his mouth and nodded. "The best I've had yet. You're a good cook."

Lucy beamed and stood to clear the dishes. "My mom taught me everything I know. She's wonderful in the kitchen."

Rand and Trey stood as well, and soon the three of them had the table cleared and the dishes in the dishwasher. Rand moved to the refrigerator, grabbed the pitcher of margarita mix and poured them all a second glass. Lucy shook her head when he handed her one. "No way. You know I can't handle more than one."

He came closer and cupped her chin in his palm, forcing her to look at him. "Let your guard down, angel. You can trust me to take care of you."

Lucy stared into a pair of the bluest eyes she'd ever seen. She'd once thought Rand wore colored contacts because the shade of his eyes just seemed too unreal. It hadn't taken her long to discover that every part of Rand was the real deal. There wasn't a single thing phony or fake about him.

She looked over at Trey, who stood to the side holding out a glass filled with the sweet, potent mixture. She surrendered. Lucy took the glass from his hands and smiled. "Fine. But if I get tipsy, it's all your fault."

"I'll take full blame if you start dancing on the kitchen table."

Lucy laughed, feeling light and free for the fist time in months. She'd been so wrapped up in worries about the future, interning for George, and wondering if she'd ever get Rand to say the three words she most craved to hear, *I love you*, that she hadn't been having any fun. It was time to shuck all the stress. Tonight she aimed to enjoy herself.

"I rented a few movies," Trey announced as they left the kitchen and entered the living room. He leaned down and grabbed two DVDs off the end table and handed them to Rand. "I hope you two like romantic comedies."

Lucy turned off the kitchen light, which only left the small table lamp illuminating the room. As she took the DVDs out of Rand's hands she realized she'd already seen one with a friend from school, but the other was new.

"Good choices," she said as she took the one she hadn't seen out of the box and put it in the player.

Rand picked up the remote and shot Trey an annoyed glare. "Dude, romantic comedies? Was all the good shit taken or what?"

Lucy smacked Rand on the arm. "It won't hurt you to watch something that doesn't involve blood and violence for once."

Rand rolled his eyes and plopped onto one end of the couch, Trey sat at the other end, which forced Lucy to sit in the middle. She took another fortifying sip of her margarita and let Rand pull her in close to his side. He wrapped an arm around her and pushed play on the remote. The movie started and they all fell silent.

Halfway into the movie, Lucy realized she'd caught maybe two minutes of it, and that was being generous. She'd been too distracted by Rand, or more specifically Rand's hands. He had one flattened high on her jean-covered thigh, and the other massaged her nape. She looked over at Trey and realized he wasn't watching the movie. He was watching her.

Rand's fingers inched higher, nearly grazing her mound. Her temperature spiked and she grabbed his hand to hold it still.

He leaned close to her ear, licked the sensitive shell, then whispered, "Let me play, angel."

She swiveled her head.

"We have company."

Rand's gaze burned into hers. "I know."

Huh? He wanted Trey to watch? "I'm not okay with this," she said, though her words lacked conviction. She meant to sound more forceful. Instead she sounded turned on.

"You sure about that?" Rand slid his palm higher, cupping her possessively. Her pussy flooded with heat as he started to stroke her clitoris through her jeans.

Lucy turned and looked at Trey. He leaned against the arm of the couch, facing them, his hands clenched into tight fists as if attempting to hold himself back. It wasn't the large erection she could see pressing against the fly of Trey's jeans that made her give Rand's hand free rein. It wasn't even the intensity in Trey's dark eyes as he stared at her as if he wanted to devour her whole. It was her own desires. She'd fantasized about both men taking her at once. She'd never dreamed it would ever happen, but here was her chance to taste the forbidden. Once in her life, every woman was given the chance to toss caution to the wind. This was her chance.

She was damned well going to take it.

She let her legs drop open, giving Rand a green light. Staring into his eyes, she saw surprise and hunger.

He kept his gaze locked on hers. "Take your clothes off, angel. Let me see that pretty body."

She sucked air into her lungs as nervous jitters flitted around in her stomach. "Rand," she murmured.

In an instant, he moved off the couch and crouched on the floor in front of her. "Relax, baby," he crooned. He started inching her yellow sweater upward, exposing her belly little bits at a time. She could only watch as Rand's gaze zeroed in on the flesh he uncovered. A muscle in his jaw jumped wildly and his gaze turned a darker shade of blue. He leaned in and kissed her lower abdomen, and then dipped his tongue into her belly button. Lucy's body responded with a flood of heat to her core. She grabbed his head and closed her eyes, relishing the sensation of his velvety tongue on her flesh.

As if floating in a dream, she felt her shirt being pulled over her head. Rand's lips never broke contact with her skin. Her bra soon followed. Now her upper half was completely bare. Her eyes flew open and she tried to cover herself as she looked over at Trey. Rand grabbed her wrists and held them at her side.

Trey hadn't moved from his position on the end of the couch. He licked his lips and watched her with hungry eyes, but he never made as if to touch her.

"He's just going to watch for a bit," Rand reassured her. "It's up to you if you want him to join us. This is for you, Lucy. You call the shots."

She was way out of her element here. She'd never taken charge during sex and she didn't know what to do. Rand had always directed their loving. When she began to protest, revealing her fears of inadequacy, Rand dipped his head and swiped his tongue over her nipple.

"Oh, God," she groaned as she relaxed her hands.

Humming his approval, he released her wrists and

sucked the hard tip into his mouth while his hand came up to massage her other breast. She was lost to the sensations flowing through her. Tingles skittered up and down her spine and her pussy throbbed, aching for relief. When he bit her gently, her hips shot off the couch. Rand pulled away, watching her closely as he released the button on her jeans and slid the zipper down. She chewed at her bottom lip when he parted the material.

"Lift your hips," he instructed.

Knowing what was about to come, Lucy raised her buttocks and let him tug her jeans down her thighs to her calves. Soon she sat with nothing but a pair of red thong satin panties covering her. Fear kept her from looking over at Trey.

Rand grinned and stroked his index finger over her clit through her panties. "You're soaked clear through, baby. You like having Trey watch us? Does it turn you on knowing he's as hard as a railroad spike right now?"

She could only speak one word in that moment. "Yes."

Rand chuckled. "Mmm, I had a feeling."

Lucy shored up her nerve and dared a glance at Trey. He grinned at her and cupped himself through his jeans. "You look good enough to eat, Lucy."

Her cheeks heated, but she didn't look away. She wasn't sure if it was the two margaritas or the look on Trey's face that made her bring her hands up to cup her own breasts in her palms. His grin slipped as he watched her fondle herself. When she pinched her own nipple, his eyes narrowed and his hands went to the button of his jeans. This time it was her turn to watch in wild fascination as Trey revealed all that power and strength to her. The chain tattoo she'd spied earlier on his forearm extended all the way up his arm, coiled around his deltoid, and ran down his pectoral muscle to link to an intricately designed red heart. She wondered about it, but as her eyes took in the rest of him, completely nude, his hand wrapped around his cock in a tight fist, she forgot all about the beautiful art work.

Lucy couldn't help comparing the two men. Trey was large. Thick veins traveled the length of his erection from balls to tip, and the swollen head was so purple it appeared painful. And delicious. She imagined suckling on him while Rand pounded into her from behind. Oh god, what if they both took her at once? She couldn't handle them both! What had she been thinking, letting things get so out of hand? She suddenly panicked and looked back at Rand, her eyes pleading with him to put a stop to things.

Rand brought his hand to her face and stroked her cheek. "You're scared and that's normal," he softly whispered. "But there's no need, baby. No one's going to hurt you. This is about pleasure, not pain."

A sudden flair of jealousy welled up as his words

registered. "You've done this before, haven't you?"

His expression hardened. "I told you before I did a lot of wild things in my younger days, Lucy. I won't lie to you. But none of that matters tonight." He slipped a single finger beneath her panties and stroked her creamy heat. "This is all that matters tonight. Pleasing this pretty little cunt is at the top of my and Trey's to-do list."

Lucy wanted to say something, anything, but she couldn't get her mouth to work for the pleasure swamping her. She watched Rand play with her beneath the red satin, his gaze daring her to take what she wanted.

"You need to trust him, Lucy," Trey said from his end of the couch.

Lucy glanced over, her eyes darting to his throbbing cock, then back to his face. She never spoke as she reached over and stroked his rock-hard thigh. She felt Rand's finger still and watched as Trey's eyes ate her up.

"Lucy." Rand's voice was filled with worry. She looked at Rand and knew in that instant that he was giving her something precious. It wasn't in his nature to share. He was much too possessive for that. He was giving her this fantasy because it was what *she* wanted. She'd thought it was impossible to love him more than she already did, but in that moment, in the dimly lit living room with two men vying for her attention, love filled her to bursting. He was her heart, her soul. She could never live without him. She knew that now.

Lucy took hold of her panties on either side of her hips and began to inch them down. Rand pulled his finger out of her and stood. As she slid the scrap of satin down her thighs, Rand undressed before her, each of them watching the other, and the moment seemed to stretch on forever. She knew then that she had very effectively surrendered, and not just to one man, but two.

Reckless Exposure: Chapter 6

Rand dropped to his knees and buried his head between her thighs. She felt his growl vibrate over her clit, and it nearly sent her over the edge. He licked her from clit to anus before sinking his tongue between her swollen pussy lips. He wrapped his strong, lean fingers around her thighs and spread her wide. Lucy moaned as he stabbed her hot opening with his tongue, then

sucked her nubbin into his mouth and flicked it with his tongue.

Another hand stroked her arm. She turned her head to see Trey beside her, his body poised and ready, and still he waited for her to make the final choice. She leaned close and kissed him gently on the lips. Trey groaned and cupped the back of her head and crushed her mouth to his. He licked the seam of her lips and coaxed her to open. She let out a sigh and Trey was there, sinking his tongue into the dark cavern of her mouth, eating at her, even as Rand slid his tongue over and around her clit.

She clutched Rand's head and smashed her pussy against his face. Rand's hands tightened around her thighs as Trey licked a fiery path down her chin to her neck. He nibbled at her sensitive skin there and moved lower to capture one puckered nipple between his teeth. His touches were more assertive than Rand's. Wilder. While Rand teased her tiny bundle of nerves, Trey bit and sucked at her breast with delicious aggressiveness.

It was as if they'd done it a million times before. Trey and Rand were in perfect harmony. Lucy could only hang on for the ride as Trey wrapped a hand around her other breast and squeezed with enough force to have her bucking and pleading. He released her nipple, and Rand sucked her clit harder, flicking and driving her body into a frenzy of need. Trey sank his mouth onto her other breast, nibbling and teasing. When Rand dipped two fingers into her heat, she lost all semblance of control. She tossed her head back and came, hard, her body drenching Rand's fingers with her cream. She cried out his name like a benediction as her body continued to convulse around him.

"Fuck yeah, baby," Rand murmured. "Come all over my hand, just like that."

Several seconds passed before Lucy was able to lift her head. She watched Rand slip his fingers free and suck her juices off. He slid his fingers inside her again and brought the drenched digits to his mouth once more, as if he couldn't get enough of her taste. She wanted to say something, to express her feelings to him, but just then Trey lifted off the couch and Rand stood. Lucy was simply too spent to move. Rand knelt down and picked her up, cradling her against his powerful chest.

"Bedroom," he said.

Too far gone to look and see, she could only assume Trey had followed.

Rand set her on her feet. When she swayed, Trey was behind her in an instant to wrap his arm around her middle and hold her steady. Rand brushed her hair from her face, kissing her lips, her cheeks, and teasing the jumpy vein in her neck.

Trey slid his hand down her stomach until he was cupping her pussy. "You're so fucking hot, Lucy." He buried his face in her hair. "You make a man want to forget about obligations. All I want to do is touch you, taste you. Fuck you."

Lucy wasn't sure what Trey meant by obligations, but as two of his large callused fingers parted her and sank deep, she couldn't force herself to care about his words. All she wanted was Rand and Trey. Both of them at once. Sinking into her. Filling her. Taking away the ache that rode her body.

Rand licked the shell of her ear, then whispered, "You owe me a blowjob, baby. Remember?"

Lucy nodded and he stepped away. She was mesmerized as Rand sat at the edge of the bed and crooked his finger at her. "Come down her, angel. Wrap those pretty lips around my dick and take me to paradise."

Trey slid his fingers out of her and stepped back. Lucy sank to her knees in front of Rand, helpless to deny his erotic request. She kept her eyes on his as she took his cock in both hands and kissed the tip. Rand snarled and wrapped a length of her dark hair around his fist. "Suck it. Don't fucking tease me right now, Lucy."

She grinned, reveling in the power surging through her. "You teased me, Rand. Turn-about is fair." She licked him from balls to tip and watched as his face turned hard with a mixture of anger and need. She was tempting the beast and she knew it, but it was so rare to see Rand lose control. Knowing it was because of her was a heady notion.

Fingers smoothed their way over her buttocks then and she turned to see Trey on his knees behind her, watching the two of them with avid interest. He danced his fingers down the cleft of her ass and Lucy's temperature spiked.

"You like it hard or gentle, Lucy?" he asked in a desire-roughened voice. "Do you like when Rand loses control and fucks this tight pussy?" His fingers caressed her entrance for emphasis. "Or would you rather draw out the pleasure? Make it last a lifetime?"

She couldn't answer, didn't dare reveal the truth to both men at once. She simply wasn't that brave. Besides, she wasn't even sure what she wanted. All she really knew was that if they didn't fill her soon, she'd surely die.

Lucy bent her head and took Rand's cock deep into her mouth, hollowing her cheeks and sucking hard on his engorged flesh.

"That's good, angel," he said. "Love that cock real sweet for me."

It was as if a barrier had dropped away. For the first time Lucy was free to explore, to take what she wanted. She cupped his balls and squeezed as she swirled her tongue over and around the bulbous head of his shaft. Rand groaned and pulled her hair. The sting at her scalp should have been a turnoff, but instead she wanted more. The pleasure-pain had her pussy weeping with need. She slipped his cock from between her lips, licked down the underside to his balls, and sucked one soft orb into her mouth.

"Jesus, baby, enough," Rand demanded. "I can't take much more."

He tried to pull her off him, but she wasn't through. She needed just one more taste of his addictive male essence. She released his balls and licked the throbbing, swollen head, moaning as the salty pre-cum hit her tongue. Lucy was so absorbed she didn't feel the caress to her buttocks a second before a hand came down, hard, connecting with her flesh. She jerked and pulled back, looking over her shoulder at a grinning Trey.

"My turn," he whispered.

She nearly melted as Trey's words registered. He remained on his knees behind her, stroking his cock in a slow rhythm that Lucy found erotic as hell. She looked at Rand for approval and he nodded. She turned and touched Trey's chest, sifting her fingers through his soft black sprinkling of hair and stroked her fingers over the heart-shaped tattoo.

Trey cursed.

Lucy looked into his face and was shocked at the savage heat she witnessed. She swirled her finger around the heart again. This time, Trey grabbed her hand in a tight hold.

"No."

Lucy frowned. "Why not?"

"It's sensitive." He appeared to have a hard time maintaining control.

Lucy let him pull her fingers away before she dipped her head and kissed his nipple. His heart beat a wild staccato against her lips. She slid her mouth upward and licked the tattoo in an exploratory motion.

He shouted her name and grabbed the back of her head. "If you want this party to end, then by all means play with the tattoo. If you want to have a little more fun, though, you're going to have to leave the damn thing alone."

Lucy had never seen anyone have such a violent reaction to a mere touch. It was as if she'd touched the head of his cock instead of his chest. Still, she wasn't about to push it. Taking him at his word, she worked her way down his torso, away from the tattoo and along the tempting trail of hair to his jutting cock.

"God, Lucy," he all but begged, "you're fucking killing me."

She laughed and wrapped her fingers around his length, his delicious width causing her to imagine him sliding into her pussy. She clenched her thighs together as the visual made her clit swell. Sliding the head of his cock between her lips, she flicked it with her tongue, encouraged by Trey's groans of approval. She teased the slit and slid him in further, suckling him gently. She felt hands on her hips and didn't know whether they were Rand's or Trey's. As the hard fingers massaged her, she realized it didn't matter.

All too soon, Trey was edging away and she was forced to stop. She whimpered.

He caressed her cheek. "You're a temptation, Lucy. Pure temptation." He stood and stepped back.

Curious what he was about, Lucy watched as he went to the bed and sprawled on his back. With his legs spread wide and one hand behind his head, his dark eyes trained on her as if she were a chocolate fudge sundae.

She glanced at Rand. He moved to the bedside table and opened the top drawer, pulling out two condoms and a tube of lubricant that she hadn't even known was there. He put the tube on the table and handed one of the condoms to Trey. Her eyes darted back and forth as she watched both powerful men sheath their more-than-impressive erections. Her mouth went dry and her heart beat so fast she was surprised it wasn't jumping right out of her chest.

Rand offered his hand and she took it. She knew what was coming. They would take her now. Nerves and excitement warred inside her. As she looked into his midnight blue eyes she saw something that brought tears to hers. Love. She didn't have to wonder at the emotion. In that moment, she saw it with total clarity. Love, not affection. Not caring. What he felt for her went soul deep. Why hadn't she seen it before?

As he led her to the bed, her thoughts scattered. She didn't know what to do, what was expected.

Trey held out his arms to her. "Come on, cover girl, climb on top. I don't bite."

She laughed as she was reminded of the way he'd nibbled on her breasts earlier. "Liar," she playfully tossed back.

He winked. "Come here."

Rand smoothed his palm over her lower back, encouraging her. "Take us both to heaven, angel."

She looked back at Rand, the need in his gaze fueling her bravado. She went up on tiptoes and kissed him. The touch of his lips, warm and soft against her own, was exactly the connection she craved. As she lifted away, Rand touched the tip of her nose. "Sweet and naughty. Trey's right, you're a temptation to any man."

Her inner vixen came to life at his words. She grinned, turned back to Trey and took his proffered hand. Trey tugged and she fell across his hard frame, the air leaving her body in a rush. He didn't give her a chance to catch her breath or second-guess her decision. He simply dove in, taking her mouth as if the devil nipped at his heels. She helplessly surrendered to his demanding lips and tongue. He slipped inside her mouth and their tongues dueled. Strong arms wrapped around her body, hugging her close. She melted, her fingers tangling in his dark tousled hair as he scoured her mouth.

Lucy felt the bed dip to one side and suddenly Rand was behind her, his palms massaging her hips and thighs.

"Think you can handle two cocks at the same time, baby?" he asked in a voice as deep and dark as sin.

Lucy wrenched her mouth from Trey's and turned her head to gaze back at Rand. "I want you, Rand," she admitted. "Both of you."

No one spoke again. Anticipation and passion arced back and forth between the three of them, their minds on what was about to take place.

A moan erupted from deep within as Rand's fingers drifted back and forth over her puckered opening. She wanted him there. Ached for him to fill her in the most taboo way.

He leaned over her and kissed the base of her spine. "Do you remember when I fucked your ass? Remember how sweet and tight it felt?"

"Yes, Rand. Oh, yes. I could never forget." Her voice had gone hoarse with need.

Trey's fingers pinched her nipples and she felt the zing of pleasure clear to her womb.

"Does the idea of having me there now, while Trey fucks your wet little pussy, turn you on?"

"You know it does," she softly whispered.

"Mmm, you're so hot, baby, you light me on fire." Rand groaned as he let his finger penetrate her, little by little, until the lubed digit was buried deep inside her anus. She shuddered and pushed against him. His finger moved in and out, fucking her with slow precision.

As Lucy started to think she could take no more of his teasing, one of Rand's big, warm hands clutched her hips. "Hold still," he ordered. She obeyed.

Suddenly Trey's sheathed cock caressed her clit, driving her mad with pleasure. Lucy writhed and moved in time to both men's strokes. When she squeezed her bottom around Rand's finger, he growled.

"None of that, baby," Rand practically pleaded. "Ease up a little for me."

She could barely concentrate on his words with Trey's cock teasing her into another climax.

"Such sweet torture you are, cover girl," Trey

murmured as he lifted his head and kissed the breast closest to his mouth.

Lucy pressed down and shuddered as his talented lips sucked in her nipple. Both breasts swelled and ached for his attention, and her sex grew damp as Rand continued to pump her ass. Soon she felt Trey slip between her swollen folds a mere inch, just enough to drive her wild. She felt every heated touch. Rand took his time, slowly sliding a single finger in and out of her ass before finally adding a second digit, stretching her, preparing her for the ultimate invasion of his cock.

Lucy flew apart, the last remnants of her inhibitions dropping away as need rushed in and took command. She gyrated against Trey while Rand tormented her from behind. When he leaned down and bit her hip, Lucy lost it.

Her climax came from out of nowhere, rising up like a flood and swamping her with a wave of wild desire. She screamed hard and loud, her back arching as her body shattered. Everything she thought she knew about sexual pleasure seemed to pale in the wake of what she'd just experienced.

Trey's rough voice just barely broke through the quagmire of her mind. "I want this pretty pussy while Rand fucks that tight ass. Will you give it to us?"

Rand growled as he slid his fingers out of her and wrapped a fist in her hair. "Look at me, angel."

She turned her head, already limp and sweating

from her second orgasm, but when she saw the intensity, the insane yearning etched into Rand's gorgeous face, her body went from sated to hungry all over again.

"You are mine," he said. "From this moment forward, you are mine."

No words sprang to mind over such a bold claim. She couldn't deal with the ramifications of it. Later, perhaps, when she wasn't out of her mind with lust.

As the heavy weight of Rand's cock pushed inside her ass, Trey nudged into her pussy. Her inner muscles clenched. She froze at the stretching pain. She panicked and tried to move away, but they were both there, two pairs of hands stroking and soothing.

"Rand, no, it's too much," she cried as her body tensed even more.

Trey pulled out instantly, lessening the pressure on the sensitive inner tissues. Rand stayed still, unmoving, barely inside the tight rim of her anus.

"Shh, it's okay," Rand crooned, "There's no hurry, baby."

"Pleasure, Lucy, only pleasure," Trey promised.

She relaxed a fraction, relieved by Rand's words and the sincerity in Trey's dark eyes.

By slow degrees Trey slid inside again, and her vagina stretched, but as he held still, pleasure began to nudge out the pain. She leaned close and buried her face against his neck. His arms came around her in a gentle hold.

"It's okay, angel," Rand said as he smoothed a palm up and down her back. "Let us take care of you. All you have to do is enjoy."

She rocked backward as Rand leaned over her, caging her in. He raked his teeth over the sensitive spot behind her ear and her panic disappeared entirely. Her body hummed back to life.

"Mmm, that's my girl. Just relax and let us take away the pain," he whispered. "Trust, remember?"

She nodded.

"You do trust him, Lucy," Trey said. "You love Rand, right?"

She lifted and stared down at Trey, deciding to give him total honesty. "More than life," she admitted, her voice rough with emotion.

His eyes softened. "Then that's all that matters."

Rand began stroking her hair and smoothing a palm downward until he cupped her bottom and kneaded the plump flesh. She melted, giving both men what they needed in that moment. Rand seemed to know the instant she submitted and began a slow glide inside her ass, filling her. There was a delicious sort of pressure and friction. Fullness. He filled her up until she thought she'd die from the sheer pleasure. But there wasn't any pain. It was like nothing she'd ever experienced. The silky inner walls of her vagina were caressed with the gentle thrusts from Trey. The forbidden nature of what they were doing sent a rush of rapture through her core.

With each inward stroke from Rand, Trey slid outward. Her muscles held them both tight and she squeezed her ass, giving Rand a small dose of the erotic pleasure-pain he craved.

Rand swore and Trey groaned. Both men's total concentration were centered on her.

Rand murmured her name and pushed against her hips, filling her completely. Trey pulled out all the way, then thrust forward. Both men stretched and filled her. Lucy's desire rose to a fever pitch, ever closer to the edge as the men thrust back and forth, fucking her with wild abandon. Her climax came over her like a tsunami, unexpected and driving her into a blissful paradise she'd never known before.

"That's good, so good. Bathe my cock with those pussy juices, Lucy," Trey murmured.

Rand pumped at her ass, fucking her hard, while Trey's slower, more precise strokes took her breath away. Suddenly both men thrust deep one last time. Lucy could feel every spasm from both their cocks as their climax took them. When they shouted her name, Lucy thought she'd never heard anything sexier.

She collapsed against Trey, exhausted, her clit still pulsing from her own orgasm, her body on fire.

Rand pulled free of her and leaned down to kiss her shoulder blade. "I do love you," he said. "More than anything in the world."

Lucy's ears were playing tricks on her, because surely he hadn't just said what she thought he said.

He brushed her damp hair from her face and kissed her cheek. "You are the best thing that's ever happened to me. No matter what you decide after tonight, I will always love you."

She forced herself to turn and look at him. For the first time, he was completely open. No barriers, no hiding behind a playful smile. And she burst into tears.

Reckless Exposure: Chapter 7

Rand stared at Lucy as tears fell down her cheeks. He'd never been comfortable when she cried. This time his heart nearly shattered as he watched her.

Trey's arms went around her in a comforting embrace, while Rand soothed her from his position atop of her. Lucy wiggled, as if to slip from between them, but Rand wouldn't let her escape. He'd just given her his heart, and she could damn well look him in the eye. "Lucy, look at me, baby," he murmured.

Lucy shook her head and buried her face against Trey's chest. If any other man had held his woman that way, Rand would have come unhinged. But Trey wasn't acting territorial. Hell, he almost acted as if he was trying to help them, as if he cared and wanted to see them work out their problems.

Rand smoothed his palm up and down Lucy's back, wishing he knew the right words to make her stop crying. But what the hell did he know about sweet words? He felt like a damn fool. He was more than shocked when Trey spoke up in his defense.

"Lucy, you need to stop this and talk to Rand," he said. "He's opening his heart to you. Don't you care about that at all?"

Lucy lifted her head and stared at Trey as if he'd grown two heads. "Care?" she asked, her voice hoarse from crying. "Are you serious?" She smacked his chest. "Men! You're all so dense! Absolutely dense!" She looked back at Rand, murder in her eyes. "Get off, or I swear I'll maim you!"

A visual of her kneeing him in the crotch sprang to mind. Rand leaped off the bed as if his ass were on fire.

Lucy was quick to follow, her stride confident as she came toward him, pointing her dainty little finger. "Four years! For four years I've been wishing you would say those words to me. What do you do? You choose the worst possible time in the world!"

"You're pissed at the timing?" His own anger shot out of control. "What the fuck does it matter *when* I tell you, as long as I tell you?"

"I was sandwiched between you and another man, you thick-headed imbecile. That's not the time to tell me—for the first time ever, mind you—that you love me!"

Rand came toward her. Lucy backed up a step and smacked into Trey, who had slipped out of bed right after she did. Lucy swiveled around, prepared to blast him too, but Trey was quicker.

"Calm down," Trey said, his voice somehow settling them both. "You wanted him to love you. He does. You wanted him to tell you his feelings out loud. He did. Give him a chance to speak before you flay him for doing the very thing you asked of him."

She crossed her arms over her chest and glared at Trey. "Don't play the counselor with me!"

"I'm not. But you need to listen to him, Lucy."

She rolled her eyes and started toward the closet. "I need clothes."

Rand and Trey watched as she crossed the room. Her sweet body seemed to glide across the carpet. She wasn't a high-paid model for nothing. Lucy exuded beauty and grace. As she donned a black silk robe, Rand nearly whimpered. He wanted her naked. Now. Every day. He'd just sated himself inside her delectable body and still he wanted to sink between her supple thighs. He looked at Trey and saw the same wild cravings in the other man's eyes. They both sighed and moved to the living room to pull on their jeans.

Partially dressed, Rand went to the kitchen and grabbed a few beers. Trey and Lucy followed close behind. He handed a cold longneck bottle to Trey and held out another for Lucy. She shook her head. Rand and Trey quickly swallowed half the contents. Lucy sat at the table and waited, her legs crossed, her fingers playing with the sash of her robe.

Rand put his beer on the counter and looked straight at the woman who held his heart. "My dad said he loved me. Then I never saw him again." Somehow the confession wasn't as hard as he'd thought it'd be. "I swore I'd never tell another living soul those three words."

She left the chair and came to him. She cupped his cheek in her soft palm. "You aren't your father. You're a good man, an honest man." Her lips thinned as she muttered, "Most days."

He covered her hand with his own. "Don't you see, Lucy? I thought he was, too. For years I thought he was perfect. I guess compared to mom, dad seemed like a saint. It took me a long time to stop watching for him at the apartment window and waiting for him to come back for me. I couldn't understand why he'd leave me."

Rand released her and pushed a hand through his hair. He went to the table, pulled out a chair, and sat down. "In the back of my mind, I sort of knew why he left mom. Even at ten years old I could see that she didn't care about herself, much less anyone else. But I couldn't let myself believe he didn't care about me. I thought he'd come back. He said he loved me. You don't abandon those you love."

Lucy started to come toward him, to comfort him no doubt, but he'd never tell her the whole story if she started touching him. He'd chicken out, as he always did. "Don't," he said. "Just let me finish."

Lucy stayed still. Trey watched him, his eyes willing him to spill his soul. "I know I told you about the way I was raised. You know about my mom and her addiction. Being so poor, we barely scraped by."

"Yes," Lucy said.

Her face was so full of love it nearly swallowed Rand whole. "Mom was controllable if she had plenty of heroin. When she ran out, she'd go through withdrawal. Those were the bad days. She'd get on these rampages, shouting and beating anything she could get her hands on. That was usually me. Dad kept her at bay most times, but even he had a hard time controlling her." He took a deep breath and went on. "After Dad left, I was defenseless. I realized damned quick that it was smart to keep mom supplied. That was the only thing that made her happy. I did whatever I could to make a buck. Sold stuff, washed windows, cleaned houses. Whatever I could to keep her satisfied."

"No kid should have to go through that. I'm sorry, Rand."

He smiled, to take the hurt out of her eyes if nothing else. "I know. It's okay. It wasn't the best way to grow up, but I survived. It sounds shitty, but when I was old enough to support myself, I got out and never looked back." He stood and went to her, unable to keep his distance any longer. Immediately her arms came around his middle and he pulled her in close, drawing strength from her in a way he couldn't with anyone else. After several seconds, he pushed back enough to see into her chocolate eyes.

"When you came along it seemed too good to be true. A sweet country girl from Ohio wanted to spend time with me. I couldn't let myself believe it would last."

"I'm just me, Rand. I'm no better or worse than you. My upbringing was good—wonderful, in fact. My parents are both loving people. But that doesn't define who I am, no more than your childhood defines you."

"I know that now. I guess I was afraid if I let myself fall in love with you, you'd leave. The thing is, I fell in love anyway. I was just too stubborn to admit it."

"I love you, Rand. I love the man you are, the child you were, and the person you'll be in the future. You're strong and smart and honest and everything I ever dreamed."

"I love you, angel. Tonight... I don't know, I thought I could let you go. I thought I could give you up. Like this would be our last hurrah or some shit. But damn, the thought of you leaving has me in knots. Give us a chance. I can give you the white picket fence and two-point-five kids if that's what you want, baby. Just don't leave."

A tear slipped down Lucy's cheek and her lower lip quivered. "Oh, Rand, I'm not going anywhere. How can I possibly leave my heart behind?" She rose up on her toes and kissed him. It was gentle, but filled with promise. She started caressing his chest as he swiped the tear away with his thumb. "There will never be another man who fills me the way you do," she swore.

"I'm bringing a load of baggage into this

relationship," he muttered, wishing like hell he could change his past.

Lucy reached down and cupped him through his jeans. She squeezed and Rand's mind went blank. "I can handle baggage. I won't break. Just love me. That's all I ever needed."

Excitement laced her words. It was music to his ears and a balm to his heart. "I do love you. I always have, baby. You own me, body and soul." He kissed her firmly, thrusting his tongue between her lips, causing her to tremble and sigh as he crushed her to him. She was giving him a chance. He wouldn't let her down.

Another voice intruded, and Rand realized he'd forgotten Trey was in the room, witnessing their tender moment.

"Since we're all happy now, any chance you two are up for an encore?"

Lucy laughed and Rand just shook his head. "Sorry, buddy. From now on, she's all mine."

Trey shrugged and moved toward them. He tugged Lucy away and Rand let her go, albeit reluctantly.

"I'll always remember you, cover girl," Trey whispered as he brushed his lips over her forehead. "Thank you, for everything."

Lucy blushed and looked down at the floor. "It was my pleasure."

Trey chuckled and smacked her ass.

Rand made a low noise in his throat and pulled Lucy

in close, tucking her under his arm where she belonged.

Trey held his hands in the air and said, "Okay, okay, I can take a hint. I'll see myself out." He started toward the living room where the rest of his clothes were strewn about.

"Hey!" Rand called after him.

Trey turned, his expression unreadable. "Yeah?"

"Are you coming over next Saturday for the game?" Rand suspected what the answer would be.

"Maybe." Tray slipped into his shirt and bent to put on his shoes. "Let's see how things go."

Rand knew he wouldn't be seeing the other man again. It was there, in his stiff posture and haunted eyes. Whatever Trey was running from, or running to, his time in New York was done.

Trey left the apartment as quietly as he'd come into their lives.

Turning to Lucy, Rand watched for signs of embarrassment over what the three of them had just experienced. He witnessed only love and acceptance on her face. He'd found his soul. The day she first walked into his studio, he should've known his life would never again be the same. "I love you, angel."

She wrapped her arms around his neck and murmured, "It's a dream come true. I've imagined this moment for so long I just want it to last forever."

"Forever, huh?" Rand smiled. "Hmm, I like the

sound of that."

"Tell me again," she pleaded. "Tell me you love me. Say it over and over while we make love."

His temperature spiked. "I will, I promise." Then he thought of the wild encounter and knew they needed to at least address it, or they'd forever avoid it. "Are you okay with everything? Any regrets?"

Lucy kissed the side of his neck. Then she bit him. His cock hardened. "No regrets," she said, her voice ringing with sincerity. "But I do think our sharing days are over, don't you?"

He thought back to his conversation with Trey, recalling the fantasy of having Lucy and another woman at once. It didn't give him the same thrill the way it once had. The only thing that gave him that type of buzz was the woman in his arms. "Yeah, our sharing days are over. You're all mine, baby."

She sighed and melted against him. "I like the sound of that."

He dipped low and slung her into his arms. He carried her to the bedroom, bypassing the bed for the bathroom. He sat her gently on the sink and turned on the shower, adjusting the water temperature. When it was perfect, he reached a hand toward Lucy.

She took it, trust and love shining in her eyes.

He took the vanilla body wash from the shelf and spent several minutes pampering her. It wasn't long before she was climaxing for him again. Afterward, he brought her to the bed where they passed the rest of the night making love.

When the morning sun filtered through the curtains, shining down on Lucy's sleeping form, Rand knew it was true. She really was an angel. A beautiful dark-haired angel, and she was all his.

Reckless Exposure: Epilogue

His thoughts on Lucy and Rand, Trey swiped a towel over his face. As always a tinge of envy shot through him. Sure, he was grateful that the couple would have their happy ending. But where did that leave him? Alone. Each time he helped another pair of lovers, he bonded with them, left a chunk of his soul behind. Lucy and Rand were no exception. They'd accepted him into their lives with open arms. He'd miss them.

A tingling sensation shot up his left arm and he looked down to see a link disappear. Another day closer to breaking the blasted curse. He should be happy. He'd helped two people find their way out of the darkness. He was that much closer to reaching his own happy ending. But he felt hollow inside.

He switched off the light and let his mind search out the pair of lovers whose bed he'd just vacated. They were in the shower, touching and talking about the future. For a second he imagined himself joining them, but he quickly banished those thoughts. That wasn't the way of things. He pushed his fingers through his hair and groaned. It was time to move on. A new city. A new couple. Perhaps a new time. Another link closer to salvation.

As he climbed into bed, he thought once more about the couple down the hall. They were loving each other. It wasn't like what he'd experienced with them. This time it was sweet, two souls touching, joining. He created a wall to shut out the beautiful images rolling through his mind.

Shit, it was going to be a long night.

About the author

Anne lives in a small town way out in the middle of no-where-ville. She is a gorgeous blonde with wonderful curves and a money tree in the backyard. Clearly, Anne is a mere figment. A ghostly figure that pops in and out of my head like a drive-by author. Nevertheless, I do so love it when she's visiting, because her imagination really is wickedly delicious! She'll bring you fantasies and erotic delights that will have you grabbing the ice water! Feel free to email Anne at anne@annerainey.com.

9 781603 105835